SWEPT AWAY BY THE ENIGMATIC TYCOON

SWEPT AWAY BY THE ENIGMATIC TYCOON

ROSANNA BATTIGELLI

MILLS & BOON

First published in Great Britain 2018
by Mills & Boon, an imprint of HarperCollins*Publishers*
1 London Bridge Street, London, SE1 9GF

Large Print edition 2018

ISBN: 978-0-263-07418-5

MIX
Paper from
responsible sources
FSC™ C007454

This book is produced from independently certified FSC™ paper to ensure responsible forest management. For more information visit www.harpercollins.co.uk/green.

Printed and bound in Great Britain
by CPI Group (UK) Ltd, Croydon, CR0 4YY

To Nic, who has always believed in me as a writer, read every draft, made delicious meals and gone along with my dreams.

Here's to a new chapter in our lives, Nic! xo

CHAPTER ONE

JUSTINE SURVEYED THE peaceful tableau lazily. The waters of Georgian Bay were calmer today, and she watched the gentle undulations with pleasure, letting her senses revel in the rugged beauty before her.

The clear blue water, shimmering with pinpoints of reflected sunlight, was dazzling—mesmerizing, really. The water lilies clustered along the water's edge looked like they were straight out of a Monet painting, their crisp white petals and yellow centers resting among dozens of flat, round, overlapping green pads. Occasionally the seagulls announced their monopoly on the sky with their shrill, almost human-like cries as they swooped and glided, tail feathers outspread, but even that wasn't enough to disrupt Justine from her contemplative mood.

She breathed in the fresh July air and congratulated herself again for exchanging the smog and humidity of the big city for *this*…this nature lover's paradise on Georgian Bay. She had made the right decision in accepting her parents' offer, Justine assured herself again as she rubbed sunscreen over her legs. Their proposal had come at the perfect time.

Working in the Toronto law office of attorney Robert Morrell had become too stressful—she'd had no choice but to resign. The memory of how she had trusted him in the first place still caused her pangs of remorse. Her mouth twisted cynically. How naïve she had been, falling for a man who was going through a turbulent divorce.

After leaving her resignation notice on his desk she had immediately headed home to Winter's Haven. As she'd pulled into the driveway, seeing her parents sitting together on the porch swing holding hands had made her burst into tears. *Why couldn't she have been so lucky?* In all her years at home she had never doubted her parents' trust, respect and devotion to each other. And to *her*. With such loving role models how could she settle for anything less?

Their love and support had cushioned her for the next four days, and then the morning she had thought herself ready to drive back to Toronto, eyes still puffy and shadowed, they'd made her an offer that took her breath away.

They had talked extensively, they'd said, and had decided that the time had come for them to retire from managing their cottage resort and to enjoy their golden years. They wanted to travel around the world while they still had their health and energy. If Justine were willing, they would sign Winter's Haven over to her and move into the smallest of the twelve cottages there. Justine could enjoy her inheritance early, and they would be delighted that the business would stay in the family.

"Take your time to think it over, sweetheart," her father had said, hugging her tightly. "But we have every confidence in your skills—business or otherwise."

Her mother had nodded and joined in the embrace, her eyes misting, and after kissing them both Justine had left, her own eyes starting to well up.

A month later the lease on her apartment had been up and she'd headed home to Winter's Haven for good.

The sting of Robert's deceit had begun to subside, and although she still had down days, feeling alternately embarrassed and angry for letting herself be fooled, she had come to terms with the end of their relationship. Taking over from her parents would occupy her time and her energy, and Justine was looking forward to exploring new ideas for the business while enjoying the more relaxed pace of the area.

Now, two months after her return, Justine could flick away any thought involving Robert almost nonchalantly. Usually followed by any number of silent declarations.

I am so over it! I'm done being a bleeding heart! Done with men and their games!

Justine closed her eyes and listened to the gentle lapping of the waves. She allowed herself to be soothed by the rhythmic sounds, enjoying the touch of the sun over her body as she settled back on the chaise longue. Tilting her sunhat to protect her face, Justine felt the familiar magic of Winter's Haven ease the stress out of her, and with a contented sigh she allowed herself to drift into a peaceful nap.

The sound of typewriter keys and a telephone

ring jolted her awake. She fumbled for her cell phone, by her side on the chaise. Squinting, she read the text.

Good God, Justine! Where the heck are you? Did you forget the two o'clock appointment I arranged for you?

Justine sat up, her heart skipping a beat. It was one fifty-five. She'd never make it in time.

She leapt up and ran the short distance from the beach to her house, not stopping until she reached the washroom on the second floor. She usually enjoyed taking leisurely showers after a soak in the sun, but on this occasion she was in and out in less than five minutes. Her shoulder-length hair would have to dry on the way there. And there was no time for make-up.

She hastily put on a flowered wrap-around skirt and a white cotton eyelet top, and made a dash to her car. She usually walked to the main office, but she wanted to avoid any further delay.

She had managed this place efficiently since her parents had turned over the business to her two months earlier. "I'll run this place as smoothly as you did," she'd promised them before they left for their retirement travels, and she had done just that—except for today.

Justine had never been late for anything in her life. She'd have to make sure it didn't happen again. It didn't make her look very responsible. She should have never given in to Mandy, who had uncharacteristically scheduled an appointment on her day off.

The sight of a sleek silver-green Mustang convertible in the parking lot dashed her hopes that her visitor might be late.

She took the steps to the office two at a time and entered the building, taking deep breaths. Mandy Holliday, her friend since high school and her assistant and office receptionist, smirked at her from behind the wooden desk, cocking an eyebrow toward the double doors leading to the diner.

"He's been waiting there thirty minutes. The last time I checked he was talking to the Elliots in Cottage Number One."

"Of all the times to doze off on the beach..." Justine grimaced. "I wonder why this Forrest man has insisted on seeing *me*. If he wants to rent a cottage, you could have dealt with him. I wish you had been able to squeeze some information out of him."

She adjusted the tie belt on her wrap-around skirt.

"I hope he's not one of those pompous business types. You know—the punctuality nuts, the arrogant *'you must be as perfect as I am'* professionals who—" She stopped at the sudden furrowing of Mandy's eyebrows.

"Perhaps you should reserve your judgment until after our meeting," a cool voice suggested directly behind her.

"I'll be in the diner if you need me," Mandy murmured, before retreating hastily.

Justine turned around stiffly to face her visitor. He was not at all what she'd expected. But what *had* she expected after hearing that ice-tinged drawl?

She tried not to reveal her surprise as her gaze smacked into the chest of his impeccably tailored gray suit before moving slowly upward to his face. His height topped hers by at least a foot. Her pulse quickened as her eyes took him in. A five o'clock shadow she suspected he wore permanently. Dark brown hair with burnished bits, styled like someone out of *GQ*. Chestnut eyes with flecks of gold.

She felt sweat on her upper lip. To her horror, she ran her tongue over her lips without thinking. She felt like combusting.

How could he look so cool in that suit? She almost felt like suggesting he remove his jacket or tie… And then her mouth crinkled slightly, nervously, at the thought of how such a suggestion would sound to him.

He caught the crooked smile, but didn't return it. He looked down at her imperiously, his jaw tense.

He's angry, Justine thought, unable to tear her gaze from his face. It was so *male* and rugged, with a straight nose and firm, sensual lips clearly visible under the meticulously groomed shadow. At second glance she caught a slight curl in his hair, and his eyes, unwavering, were disturbingly hypnotizing.

"I'm sorry," she said quickly. "I didn't mean to offend you. I was irritated at myself for being late. It's not like me." She extended her hand, forcing herself to offer him an apologetic smile. "I'm Justine Winter."

For a moment, he just stared at her, and Justine was about to withdraw her hand in embarrassment when he finally took it, his long fingers closing around hers completely in a firm clasp.

"Apology accepted," he replied, motioning abruptly for Justine to sit down.

She did so and he pulled up a nearby chair.

"What can I do for you, Mr. Forrest?"

"Forrester. Casson Forrester."

Her eyebrows shot up at his name. "Yes, of course. You made an appointment with Mandy to see me, but you didn't state your reasons. Are you interested in renting a cottage? Did you want a tour of the grounds and facilities before making a reservation? We may have an opening, depending when it is you want to stay." She paused, realizing she was babbling.

His lips curved slightly. "Yes, I'm very interested in the cottages. You see, I've just purchased the adjoining land on both sides of your property."

Justine frowned. "I can't believe the Russells have sold their properties—" She broke off, stunned. The Russells' ancestors had been among the original homesteaders in the area.

"I made them a convincing offer." He was unable to conceal the satisfaction in his voice. "Our transaction was mutually profitable."

Justine looked at him warily. "I don't suppose you arranged this appointment just for the sake of meeting your new neighbor...?"

He laughed curtly. "You're perceptive, if nothing else."

Justine flushed, her mouth narrowing. She didn't like the negative implication of "if nothing else." "Why don't you come right to the point?" she suggested sweetly, trying not to clench her teeth.

His eyebrows arched slightly at her directness. "I have development plans for both lakefront properties," he explained brusquely. "However, *your* property, being in the center, poses a number of problems for me. It would seem that the ideal solution would be for me to purchase this property in order to maximize the success of my venture." His eyes narrowed. "Just name your price. You'll have it in your bank account first thing tomorrow morning."

Justine couldn't prevent the gasp from her lips. "You can't be serious!"

"I'm not the joking type," he countered sharply. "Nor do I intend to play any money games with you, Miss Winter. Negotiations aren't necessary here. I'm willing to pay whatever you feel is an optimum price for this place."

Justine felt her eyes fluttering in disbelief. "I'm not interested in selling—no matter what you offer, Mr. Forrester," she stated as firmly as she could muster. "It's not a matter of money; it's a question of principle."

She stood up, both palms on the table, willing him to leave.

A muscle flicked at his jaw. He made no move to stand, let alone leave. "Kindly explain yourself, Miss Winter," he said evenly.

Justine took a deep breath. "I would not want to see the natural beauty and seclusion of this area spoiled by a commercial venture. That's what you have in mind, don't you?" She put her hands on her hips, her blue-gray eyes piercing his accusingly.

"Let me clarify my intentions."

He leaned forward, resting both elbows on Justine's desk. His face was disturbingly close to her chest. She was mortified as she noticed her black bra peeking from under the white eyelet blouse. She hadn't even thought about the selection of her bra in her after-shower haste. She sat down and crossed her arms in front of her.

"I think the rugged beauty of this stretch of Georgian Bay shoreline should be fully enjoyed—not kept a secret. I am contemplating the construction of a luxury waterfront resort and a restaurant that will enhance the experience of visitors. Nothing like high-rise condominiums; that would be unnatural in these surroundings."

He rubbed his jaw with long, manicured fingers.

"I like the thought of luxury cottages nestled privately among the pines and spruces, each overlooking the bay." He paused briefly, but as she opened her mouth to reply, added coolly, "Let me make one thing clear, Miss Winter. Even if you refuse to accept my offer, I intend to go ahead with my plans for the Russell properties."

Justine had listened with growing trepidation as she thought of the repercussions his commercial venture would have—not only on her property, but on the surrounding area. She had no intention of giving in to him. His plans would *not* enhance the existing atmosphere of this stretch of the bay—she was certain of it. The seclusion and quiet ambiance her customers depended on would definitely be compromised with all the construction and traffic his venture would generate.

She felt her jaw clenching. No, she did not intend to let him bully her into selling.

"I cannot accept your offer," she told him coldly. "*Someone* has to cater to common folk with regular incomes who want a holiday away from it all. I cannot, in all good conscience, agree to a proposal that would not only deprive my regular customers of a quiet, restful vacation retreat, but also exploit the natural wilderness of the area."

She was unable to control a slight grimace.

"Have you even thought of looking into the Georgian Bay Biosphere Reserve? Or the Provincial Endangered Species Act? Obviously, Mr. Forrester, personal financial gain is higher on your list of priorities than the preservation of nature."

Justine stood up again, hoping he would take the hint and leave.

Instead he leaned back in his chair and continued to gaze directly at her, an unfathomable gleam in his chestnut eyes. She cleared her throat uncomfortably, wondering what she could say to get him out of the office without resorting to being rude.

Stroking his jaw thoughtfully, he murmured, "Why don't I just make you an offer anyway? How does this sound to you…?"

Justine only just stopped herself from swaying. Even half the amount he was offering would be exorbitant. No wonder the Russells had sold out to him if this was the way he conducted his business transactions. For a moment her mind swarmed with thoughts of what she could do with that kind of money, and she couldn't deny that she felt the stirrings of temptation to consider his offer.

She looked at him, sitting back comfortably with his arms crossed, and the hint of smugness on his face gave her the impression that he knew exactly what she was feeling. He was counting on it that she would abandon her principles if the price were right.

Well, he was *wrong*. She might have been

tempted in a moment of weakness, but she would never sell Winter's Haven. It represented a lot of things for a lot of people, but for her it was *home*. Her special healing place. Even her hurt over Robert had lessened since she had come back. There was an atmosphere here that she had never felt in the city—or anywhere else for that matter. She had an affinity for this kind of natural lifestyle, and after leaving it once she had no intentions of ever leaving it again.

Her blue-gray eyes were defiant as she looked across at him. "I'm sorry, Mr. Forrest…"

"Forrester."

"Mr. *Forrester*. I can imagine that your offer might be tempting to some, but nothing would make me sell my home and property. I belong here."

Surprise flickered briefly in the depths of his eyes. "Bad timing."

"What do you mean?" she demanded defensively.

"Your parents were almost ready to accept an offer I made on this place three months ago, then changed their minds when you showed up. It's too bad for me that you didn't time your arrival for a week later. The deal would have gone through by then," he continued bluntly, "and I wouldn't have had to waste my valuable time talking to you."

He rose fluidly from the chair.

Justine could feel her cheeks flaming. She remembered her parents mentioning an offer somebody had made—it hadn't been the first time—but that they had turned it down.

"What's *really* too bad, *Mr. Forrester*," she shot back indignantly, "is the fact that you've become my neighbor."

He smiled, but the smile didn't reach his eyes. "Not for long, perhaps," he replied coolly. "I will come up with another offer soon—one you may not be able to resist, despite your lofty principles."

"Don't count on it," she snapped.

"We'll see," he replied softly. "Any woman can eventually be bought. I don't imagine you're any different." He turned to leave with a cynical smile. "Except maybe a little higher-priced," he said, his tone cold as he opened the door and clicked it shut.

Justine stared at the door speechlessly. She

slammed one palm down on the desk, furious that he had had the last word—and the last insult.

"Ouch," she moaned, slumping into her chair.

She felt emotionally drained. The last thing she had expected from her visitor today was an offer to buy Winter's Haven. *And what an offer,* she mused.

Casson Forrester obviously meant business, and money was no object. She didn't imagine he would stop at anything until ultimately he got what he wanted. And he wanted Winter's Haven. He hardly seemed the type to back away from any venture once he had made up his mind.

Justine recalled the set of his jaw and the steely determination in his eyes. Those dangerous tawny eyes. Tiger eyes, she thought suddenly, eyes that made her feel like the hunted in a quest for territorial supremacy.

How long would he stalk her? she wondered nervously, rubbing at her sore palm. What means would he use to try to break down her resolve and get her to give in to him?

It doesn't matter what he tries, an inner voice reasoned. *There's nothing he can do to make you change your mind.*

"Nothing!" She rose to leave.

At that moment Mandy returned to the office, unconcealed curiosity on her face. "What do you mean, '*Nothing*'? Tell me what that hunk of a man wanted… Please say he's booked a cottage for a month. I'll be more than happy to forego my vacation and tend to his every need—"

"He's not worth getting excited about," Justine sniffed. "He's an assuming, boorish snob who thinks money can buy anything or anyone." She felt her cheeks ignite with renewed anger. "He's got a lot of nerve."

"I take it you didn't quite hit it off?" Mandy said, sitting on the edge of the desk. "What on earth did he say—or do—to get you so riled up? I've never seen this side of you."

"That's because no one has ever infuriated me so much," Justine huffed.

She told Mandy the purpose of Casson Forrester's visit.

"I'll never sell, though," she concluded adamantly. "To him or to anyone else."

"Hmm…it doesn't sound like we've heard the last of him, though, since he *is* our new neighbor." A dreamy look came into her eyes. "I wonder if he's married..."

"I pity his wife if he is," Justine retorted. "Having to live with such an overbearing, narrow-minded brute!"

"I'd like to see what your idea of a hunk is if you consider this man a brute!" Mandy laughed.

Justine gave an indelicate snort. "All that glitters isn't gold, you know. He may look...*attractive*—"

"Gorgeous," Mandy corrected.

"But it's the inside that counts. Trust me, Mandy, he has a *terrible* personality. No, it's not even terrible. It's non-existent."

Mandy eyed her speculatively. "Not your kind of man?"

"Not at all," Justine replied decisively, turning to leave. "If he calls again, think up any excuse you can; just tell him I'm not available. Whatever you do, *do not* set up another appointment. I've had enough personal contact with Casson Forrest... Forrester—whatever his name is—to last me a lifetime. All I want to do is forget him."

Easier said than done, she thought, driving the short distance back to her house. How could she forget those tiger eyes? His entire face, for that matter… It was not a face one could easily forget. Not that *she* was interested, but she had to admit grudgingly to herself that Casson Forrester probably never lacked for female companionship.

Or lovers, she mused, stepping out of her car. She felt a warm rush as she imagined him in an intimate embrace, then immediately berated herself for even allowing herself to conjure such thoughts.

Justine sprinted up the stairs to her bedroom, changed into her turquoise swimsuit, grabbed a towel, and headed to her private beach.

The first invigorating splash into the bay immediately took some of her tension away. And as Justine floated on the bay's mirrored surface, absorbed in interpreting the images in the clouds, the threat that Casson Forrester posed to Winter's Haven already seemed less imposing.

What vacationers liked most about the place was the seclusion of each of the twelve rustic cottages tucked amidst the canopy of trees, only a short walk to their own stretch of private beach. They also appreciated the extra conveniences that Justine's parents had added to enhance their stay.

Along with the popular diner—which featured freshly caught pickerel, bass or whitefish—over seventeen years her parents had added a convenience store, a small-scale laundromat, and boat and motor facilities with optional guiding services.

Many of their guests came back year after year during their favorite season. Justine hoped that Casson Forrester's plans wouldn't change that.

She swam back to shore, towel-dried her hair, patted down her body quickly and decided she would change and eat at the diner instead of cooking. She liked to mingle with the guests, many of whom had become friends of the family.

Justine put on her flip-flop sandals, hung up her towel on the outside clothesline, and walked up the wide flagstone path. On either side myriad flowers bloomed among Dusty Millers and variegated hostas.

Ordinarily Justine entered through the back entrance after going for a swim, but the sound of tires crunching slowly up toward the front of her house made her change her mind. A new guest, she thought, mistaking her driveway for the office entrance.

She rounded the corner with a welcoming smile. The car sitting in her driveway had tinted windows, so she couldn't make out the driver. But she didn't have to. Her smile faded and she stopped walking. She knew who the silver-green Mustang convertible belonged to.

With the windows up he had full advantage, seeing her with her swimsuit plastered to her body, hair tousled and tangled. She wished she had wrapped her towel around her.

She felt her insides churn with annoyance. Frustration.

Was he going to come out of his car, or did he actually expect her to walk up to his window?

She stood there awkwardly, her arms at her sides, feeling ridiculous. Just when she thought she couldn't stand it anymore, the convertible top started to glide down. Spanish guitar music was playing.

He had shades on, which annoyed her even further. He had taken off his jacket and tossed it on the seat beside him. His shirt was short-sleeved, and even from where she stood Justine could tell it was of high quality, the color of cantaloupe with vertical lime stripes. His arms were tanned, and she watched him reach over to grab a large brown envelope, turn down the music slightly and step out of his car. Without taking his gaze off her.

"I wanted you to have a glance at this, Miss Winter." He held out the envelope.

Justine crossed her arms and frowned.

"It's a development proposal drafted by an architect friend of mine. I would be happy to go over it with you." When she didn't respond, he added, "I would appreciate it if you at least gave the plan and the drawings a glance. They might help dispel some of your doubts about my venture."

Justine stared at him coldly. "I'm not interested, Mr. Forrest. You're wasting your time." Her entire face felt flushed, the refreshed feeling after her swim completely dissipated.

He stood there for a moment, his mouth curving into a half-smile. He held the envelope in front of her for a few moments, then turned and tossed it into the Mustang. "Very well, Miss *Wintry*. Perhaps you need some time to think about it."

"Not at all," she returned curtly. "And my last name is *Winter*."

"So sorry, Miss *Winter.*" He took off his sunglasses. "And mine's *Forrester.*"

Justine's knees felt weak. His dark eyes blazed at her in the sunlight. She knew she should apologize as well, but when she opened her mouth no words came out. She watched him get behind the wheel and put on his sunglasses.

"But you can call me Casson," he said, and grinned before turning on the ignition.

He cranked up the music and with a few swift turns was out of her driveway and out of sight.

Now that he could no longer see Justine Winter in his rearview mirror, Casson concentrated on the road ahead. He loved this area. His family—which had included him and his younger brother Franklin—had always spent part of the summer at their friends' cottage on Georgian Bay, and the tradition had continued even after they'd lost Franklin to leukemia when he was only seven years old.

Even after his parents and their friends had passed away, and the cottage had been sold, Casson had felt compelled to return regularly to the area. There would always be twinges of grief at his memories, but Casson didn't want the memories to fade, and the familiar landscape brought him serenity and healing as well.

Determined to find a location for what would be "Franklin's Resort," he had spent months searching for the right spot. After finding out that the Russell properties were for sale, he'd hired a pilot to fly him over Georgian Bay's 30,000 Islands area to scope out the parcels of land, which were on either side of Winter's Haven.

The seductive curve of sandy beach, with the surf foaming along its edge, and the cottages set back among the thickly wooded terrain had given him a thrill. The bay, with its undulating waves of blue and indigo, sparkling like an endless motherlode of diamonds, had made his heartbeat quicken.

The sudden feeling that Franklin was somehow with him had sent shivers along his arms. Casson had always sensed that the spirit of Franklin was in Georgian Bay, and he'd had an overwhelming feeling that his search was over. He'd made the Russells an offer he was sure they couldn't refuse and had then turned his attention to Winter's Haven.

Now, as he sped past the mixed forest of white pine, birch and cedar, he caught glimpses of Georgian Bay, its surface glittering with pin-points of sunlight. A mesmerizing blue.

Just like Justine Winter's eyes.

The thought came before he could stop it. His lips curved into a smile. He hadn't expected the new owner of Winter's Haven to be so…*striking.* So outspoken. From the way her father had spo-ken he had expected someone a little more shy and reticent, someone more *fragile.*

"I've decided not to sell after all," Thomas Win-ter had said, when he'd phoned him a few months earlier. "My daughter Justine has had enough of the big city—and a bad relationship—and she needs a new direction in life. A new venture that will lift her spirits. My wife and I have decided to offer the business to her and finally do some travelling. Winter's Haven will be a good place for Justine to recover…"

Recover?

Casson had wondered if Mr. Winter's daugh-ter was emotionally healthy enough to maintain a business that had obviously thrived for years under her parents' management. Which was why he'd decided to wait a couple of months before approaching her with his offer. With any luck the place would be in a shambles and she'd be ready to unload it. And even if that wasn't the case, he'd come to learn that most people had their price…

At first glance Justine Winter had seemed anything but fragile. She had dashed into the office with damp hair, flushed cheeks, tanned arms and shapely legs under a flowered skirt that swayed with the movement of her hips. And as he'd sauntered toward her his eyes hadn't been able to help sweeping over that peekaboo top, glimpsing the black bra underneath…

He had felt a sudden jolt. He had come to Winter's Haven expecting a depressed young woman who had needed her parents to save her by offering her a lifeline. *Not a woman whose firm curves and just-out-of-the-shower freshness had caused his body to stir uncontrollably...*

And then she had turned to face him, her blue-gray eyes striking him like a cresting wave. And, no, it *hadn't* looked like the place was anywhere near in a shambles, with her pining away for her former lover.

He had watched her expression flit from disbelief about his purchase of the adjoining Russell properties to wide-eyed amazement at his offer. And he had felt a momentary smugness when her gaze shifted and became dreamy.

She had been thinking about what she could do with the money. He'd been sure of it.

And then her gaze had snapped back to meet his, and the ice-blue hardness of her eyes and her flat-out refusal of his money had caused something within him to strike back with the prediction that she would eventually cave at a higher price.

He had almost been able to feel the flinty sparks from her eyes searing his back as he'd left…

Casson drove into the larger of the Russell properties—*his* properties now—and after greeting his dog, Luna, he grabbed a cold beer and plunked himself down into one of the Muskoka chairs on the wraparound porch.

Luna ran around the property for a while and then settled down beside him. Casson stared out at the flickering waters of the bay. It already felt like he had been there for years.

This really was a slice of heaven. Prime Group of Seven country.

Casson had grown up hearing about the Group of Seven as if they were actual members of his family. His grandfather's friendship with A. J. Casson—who had been his neighbor for years—and the collection of Casson paintings he had eventually bequeathed to his only daughter, had resulted in Casson's childhood being steeped in art knowledge and appreciation. Not only of A. J. Casson's work, but the work of all the Group of Seven artists.

And now here he was as an adult, just days away from sponsoring and hosting Franklin & Casson on the Bay—an exhibition of the paintings of Franklin Carmichael and A. J. Casson at the Charles W. Stockey Centre for the Performing Arts in Parry Sound. The center was renowned for its annual Festival of the Sound summer classical music festival, as well as for housing the Bobby Orr Hall of Fame—a sports museum celebrating Parry Sound's ice hockey legend.

It was all close to falling into place. This exhibition was the first step in making his resort a reality. Franklin's Resort would be a non-profit venture, to honor the memory of its namesake and to provide a much-needed safe haven for families.

At the exhibition Casson would outline his plan to create a luxury haven for children after cancer treatment—a place to restore their strength and their spirit with their families, who would all have experienced trauma. The families would enjoy a week's stay at the resort at no cost.

He had no doubt that the Carmichael/Casson exhibition would be successful in raising awareness and backing for his venture. And the *pièce de résistance* was a painting from his own personal collection. It was one of A.J. Casson's early pieces, *Storm on the Bay*, and had been given to Casson's grandfather when A.J. had been his neighbor. It was the prize in a silent auction, and Casson hoped it would attract a collector's eye and boost the development of the resort.

A lump formed in his throat. He had been only ten when Franklin had died, and although he had not been able to articulate his feelings at the time, he knew now that he had coped with his feeling of helplessness by overcompensating in other ways. Helping with chores; learning to make meals as a teen and excelling at school, in sport and at university. Subconsciously he had done everything he could not to add to his parents' misery.

After pursuing a Business and Commerce degree in Toronto, Casson had returned home to Huntsville—an hour away from Parry Sound—to purchase a struggling hardware store downtown. He had been grateful for the money his grandfather had left him in his will, which had enabled him to put a down payment on the business, and he'd vowed that he would make his grandpa proud.

Within a couple of years the store had been thriving, and Casson had set his sights on developing a chain. Six more years and he'd had stores in Gravenhurst, Bracebridge, Port Carling and—his most recent acquisition—a hardware store in Parry Sound, just outside the Muskoka area.

Casson had revived each store with innovative changes and promotions that would appeal both to the locals and the seasonal property-owners. The Forrest Hardware chain had made him a multi-millionaire by the time he was thirty-four.

Losing his brother at such a young age had affected Casson deeply; he hadn't been able to control what happened to Franklin, so he had learned to take control of his own life early. He was still in control now, steering his expanding hardware chain, and yet he had no control over Justine Winter. Not that he wanted to control *her*; he simply wanted control of Winter's Haven. Her property was the last piece of the puzzle that he needed to fit into his plan.

Earlier, the thought had flashed into his mind to invite Justine to go with him to the Stockey Centre the following day—to show her that his motive when it came to the Russell properties and Winter's Haven was not one of financial gain, as she had immediately assumed. However, the fact that he'd even considered telling Justine the truth shocked him… He *never* talked about Franklin. He'd learned to keep those feelings hidden.

Why had he nearly told her?

It might have had something to do with those initial sparks between them…

Anyway, he hadn't wanted to show his vulnerability or how much this venture meant to him as a tribute to his brother. So instead he had thrust his offer upon Justine with the arrogant expectation that she would be so dazzled by the amount she'd agree to it, no questions asked.

And if she *had* asked questions he wouldn't have been prepared to open up his soul to her. Tell her that he was doing this not only for Franklin, but for himself. For all the lonely years he had spent after his brother's death, unable to share his grief with his mother, whose pain at losing Franklin had created an emotional barrier that even Casson could not penetrate. His father had thrown himself into his work, and when he was at home had seemed to have only enough energy to provide a comforting shoulder for his wife.

It was only in later years that Casson had contemplated going to a few sessions of grief counselling. It had been emotionally wrenching to relive the past, but Casson had eventually forgiven his parents. It had been during that time that his idea for a resort to help kids like Franklin had begun to take root. What he hadn't been able to do for Franklin at ten years of age, he could now do for many kids like him—including his godson Andy, his cousin Veronica's only child.

Andy's cancer diagnosis a year earlier had shocked Casson, and triggered memories and feelings of the past. Supporting Andy and Veronica during subsequent treatment had made him all the more determined to see his venture become a reality. Casson just wished his parents were still alive to witness it as well…

Franklin & Casson on the Bay was only a few days away. His plan was on target. There was one key missing.

And Justine had it.

Casson took a gulp of his beer. *Damn*, it was hot. He loosened his tie. As he contemplated changing and going for a swim, a vision of Justine Winter standing with wet hair in her bathing suit flashed in his memory. That turquoise one-piece had molded to the heady curves of her body, and her tanned thighs and legs had been sugared with white beach sand that sparkled in the sun. Her hair, straight and dripping water over her cleavage… An enchanting sea creature…

He had sensed her discomfort, knew how exposed she'd felt. If only she knew what the sight of her body had done to *him*.

Casson unbuttoned his shirt and went inside to change. A dip in the refreshing waters of Georgian Bay would cool him down—inside and out…

* * *

Casson stretched out on the edge of the dock to let the sun heat his body. There was nothing like that first dive into the bay when your body was sizzling hot. He closed his eyes for a few moments, and when he opened them, wondered if he had dozed off. Although he had slapped on some sunscreen earlier, his skin felt slightly more burnished.

He scrambled to his feet and Luna shuffled excitedly around him. Casson heard a faint voice calling him, but when he turned there was nobody there. There was some rustling in the trees and a flash of blue, followed by the shrill call of a blue jay.

Casson looked down at the water, anticipating the bracing pleasure awaiting him. A hint of a breeze tickled his nose, followed by the faint smell of fish. He blinked at his reflection, wiping at the sweat prickling his eyes. In the gently lapping bay he imagined Franklin beside him, wearing his faded Toronto Blue Jays cap, his skinny arms holding a fishing rod with its catch of pickerel and his toothy grin. And the sparkle in his eyes…

And then the sparkle was lost in the sun's glittering reflection and the image was swallowed up by the waves. Casson dropped down to sit at the edge of the dock, his original intention forgotten. He continued to peer intensely into the water, and it was only moments later, when Luna pressed against him to lick his face, that Casson realized she was licking the salty tears on his cheeks.

CHAPTER TWO

THE RAIN DRUMMING on the roof woke Justine an hour before she'd intended. She didn't mind at all, though. Rainy days were good for doing odd jobs, renovating an empty cottage, or just relaxing with a good book in the window seat in her room. It was one of her favorite reading spots, with its plush flowery cushions and magnificent view of the bay.

Justine changed into jeans and a nautical-style T-shirt, brushed her hair back into a ponytail, and went downstairs. After having a quick coffee and one of the banana yogurt muffins she had made last night, she grabbed her umbrella and dashed to her car.

Despite the fact that she had always liked this kind of weather, Justine couldn't help but feel a twist in her stomach, remembering the rainy day she'd walked into Robert Morrell's law office for an interview. She'd been twenty-four, and had graduated *summa cum laude* in Law and Justice from the University of Toronto. That and her business electives had impressed Robert and Clare, his senior administrative assistant, who would be retiring in six months, and Robert had offered her the job the following day.

As time had progressed the initial rapport between them had developed into an easy friendship. Justine had sometimes stayed at the office during lunchtime, catching up on paperwork between bites of her sandwich or salad. And Robert, to her surprise, had often done the same, claiming he wanted to go home at a decent hour so his wife wouldn't complain that he was "married to the job."

Shared conversations had begun to take on a more personal note during Justine's second year at the office, and when Robert had started to hint at his marriage breakdown she had felt compelled to listen and comfort him as he'd revealed more and more.

The underlying spark of attraction between them had not come to the forefront until after his divorce had almost become final. Then, with nothing and nobody to hold them back, Justine and Robert had begun dating…

Justine forced Robert out of her thoughts as she turned the corner and drove into the parking lot of the hardware store, finding a spot near the front doors. Something looked vaguely different about the place, and then she realized the signage had changed. New ownership, she had heard.

Without bothering to get her umbrella, she dashed into the store and toward the wood department.

"May I help you?"

Justine turned to find a middle-aged employee smiling at her.

"Yes, thank you, Mr. Blake," she said, smiling back. "Glad to see you're still here. I'd like to order some cedar paneling for one of the cottages."

"I thought it was you. Back from Toronto, I hear. Your dad told me you'd be taking over Winter's Haven."

Justine nodded. "I'm glad to be back."

As she handed him a piece of paper with the measurements a feeling of contentedness came over her. She *had* made the right decision, coming back home.

This was what she loved about living in a small town—knowing the names of local merchants, dealing with people who knew her parents.

She had felt the call of the big city, and had enjoyed it for a time, but the breakup with Robert and the lonely month that had followed had made her realize how truly *alone* she was. With no job and no meaningful friendships—the people Robert had introduced her to didn't qualify—she'd yearned for the small-town connections of Parry Sound. *Home.* The place she had always felt safe in, nurtured and supported by family, friends and community.

"Are you thinking of running the business on a permanent basis?" Mr. Blake glanced at her curiously.

"I sure am." She beamed. "I can't imagine ever leaving Winter's Haven again."

Mr. Blake glanced over her shoulder, as if he were looking for someone, and then gave her a hesitant smile. "Well, good luck to you. When your order is ready I'll give you a call. You can let me know then when you want the job done."

"Sounds good!" Justine leafed through her bag and took out her car keys. "Thanks, Mr. Blake, and have a great day."

Justine strode toward the exit, wondering why the expression on his face had seemed to change after her saying she couldn't imagine ever leaving Winter's Haven. She grimaced when she came to the door. The rain was coming down in torrents now, and she regretted leaving her umbrella in the car. She would get drenched despite the short distance.

She made a run for it, giving a yelp as she stepped in a sizeable puddle.

"Damn," she muttered as she inserted the wrong key in the lock. She should have brought a rain jacket, she berated herself, slamming the door at last.

Her top was plastered against her, and although she had planned to do some further shopping she was not about to go anywhere in this condition. Her jeans were soaked as well—front and back—and she couldn't wait to get back home, strip everything off and take a shower.

She backed out carefully and drove out of the parking lot. Although it was barely mid-morning the sky had darkened, and she could hear ominous rumbles of thunder. Her wipers were going at full-tilt, but the rain was pelting the windshield so hard that she could barely see through it.

As Justine drove slowly out of the town limits and toward the long country road that would take her home she tried to ignore the clammy feeling of her wet clothes against her skin.

A sudden beeping noise behind her startled her, and she glanced immediately in the rearview mirror. She could see a burgundy pickup truck, but it was impossible to see the driver.

To Justine's consternation the honking became more persistent. The truck didn't have its indicators on, so the driver couldn't be in any kind of trouble. And she didn't imagine it was an admirer. She wasn't unused to appreciative smiles from male drivers once in a while, along with the occasional whistle or honk of their horn, but she doubted that this was the case today.

The rain was subsiding—thank goodness. And as she looked in the rearview mirror again she saw that the driver had his arm out the window, signaling for her to pull over. Now she felt alarmed. Was it a cop? No, not in a pickup truck. And it wouldn't be for speeding…

He honked again and she looked back, but a sudden rush of oncoming cars made her concentrate on the road. She cautiously pressed on the gas pedal. *Too many weirdos on the road,* she thought. She swerved around a bend, and a quick look reassured her that the creep was gone.

She reached the turnoff to Winter's Haven. The rain had stopped and the sun was breaking through the clouds. She clicked off her wipers, headed directly past the office building and turned into the road through a lengthy wooded stretch that led to her driveway. She sighed, but had barely turned off the ignition when she heard the crunch of an approaching vehicle.

A moment later the burgundy pickup truck she'd thought she had seen the last of pulled up right next to her.

She was more angry than worried now. *How dare he?* Without a thought to any potential danger, she flung the car door open and got out, her cheeks flaming. The man had gotten out of his truck and was leaning against it, casually silent, as he watched Justine march stormily up to him.

"Why are you following me?" she demanded, stopping a few feet away from him. "It was bad enough trying to drive with you tailgating and honking incessantly. Can't you find a more civilized way of pursuing a woman? Highway dramatics don't do anything for me."

The man's mouth twisted and he continued to stare at her through dark sunglasses. A few seconds passed. Why wasn't he answering her? Maybe she should have stayed in the car. He might have a knife. She could scream, but nobody was close enough to hear her.

She looked at him closely. She might need to file a report if she managed to get away from him. His faded jeans and jacket seemed ordinary enough, but his bearded face, dark glasses and baseball cap might very well be concealing the face of an escaped criminal. Would she be able to run back to her car? No, she'd never make it if he intended to pursue her.

She shivered and said shakily, "What do you want?"

Another twist of his lips. "Your hubcap flew off a few miles back," he drawled. "So you can relax. I'm not about to attack you."

Justine let out an audible sigh. And then she felt her cheeks start to burn. She had accused him of *pursuing* her.

"I'm usually more civilized when it comes to pursuing women," he said, and laughed, as if he had read her thoughts. "And 'highway dramatics,' as I believe you put it, are not my style."

Justine's discomfiture grew. "I apologize for jumping to the wrong conclusion, but you can hardly blame me, can you?" Her eyes narrowed. "Your voice sounds familiar..."

For some reason, the realization bothered her. A suspicion suddenly struck her in a way that made her knees want to buckle.

"Haven't figured it out yet?" he said, removing his sunglasses.

Tiger eyes. Damn!

With the cap, sunglasses, casual clothes and truck, and two weeks' growth of beard, she hadn't even suspected.

"It's...*you*!" she sputtered, wide-eyed.

"Nice to see you again, too," Casson Forrester murmured, with the slightest hint of sarcasm. "Actually, I spotted you in the hardware store, but you left before I could reach you. There are a few things I want to discuss with you."

"You didn't have to follow me."

"I didn't think you'd accept my call." His eyes narrowed. "Among other things, I was going to suggest you don't bother paneling or doing any other kind of work if you're going to end up selling the place..."

Justine's eyes flashed their annoyance. "That's your mistaken presumption," she retorted. "And were you eavesdropping on my conversation?"

"I didn't have to. Mr. Blake happened to mention it when I called a staff meeting."

"You *own* Forrest Hardware?" she said slowly. "And Forrest Construction...."

Of course. Forrest was simply an abbreviated form of his name, and an appropriate choice for his chain of stores in the Muskoka area—including the latest one in Parry Sound. She had briefly noticed the new sign, but the name hadn't registered in her consciousness—least of all the connection with its owner.

She gave a curt laugh. "No wonder you can buy practically anything—or anybody—you want."

"Not always," his tiger eyes glinted. "Although it's not for lack of trying."

She shivered. And at the sudden clap of thunder they both looked up to the sky. The clouds had blocked out the sun again, and a few errant raindrops had started coming down. Realizing she had been standing there in her wet T-shirt and jeans, her hair flattened against her head except for the few strands that were now curling with the humidity, she crossed her arms in front of her.

"Excuse me," she said icily, "I'm going to have to leave." She turned away, then glanced back. "I'll look for the hubcap later."

She retrieved her keys and bag from her car and strode toward the house. When she was halfway there the rain intensified, making her curse indelicately as she ran the rest of the way. Breathing a sigh of relief as she reached the door of the porch, she closed it behind her as another clap of thunder reverberated around her.

Hearing the porch door creak open again, she turned around to close it tightly. But it wasn't the wind that had forced it open. It was Casson Forrester. And a big dog.

"I hope you don't mind if we wait out the storm

in your house." He closed the porch door firmly. "Driving would be foolish in almost zero visibility. And Luna is terrified of storms." He took off his cap and grinned at Justine. "Would you be so kind as to hand me a towel? I'd hate for us to drip all over your house."

Justine blinked at the sight before her. Casson Forrester and his big panting dog, both dripping wet.

Casson took off his baseball cap and flung it toward the hook on the wall opposite him. It landed perfectly. He looked at her expectantly, one hand in a pocket of his jeans, the other patting Luna on the head. Both pant legs were soaked, along with his jean jacket.

She tore her gaze away from his formfitting jeans and looked at Luna. She'd make a mess in her house, for sure. She sighed inwardly. Did she have any choice but to supply this dripping duo with towels? She couldn't very well let them stand there.

Anther clap of thunder caused Luna to give a sharp yelp, and she rose from her sitting position, looking like she wanted to bolt.

Justine blurted, "I'll just be a minute," and hurried inside, closing the door with a firm click. She wasn't going to let either of them inside until they were relatively drip-free.

She scrambled up the stairs to the hall closet near her room, fished out a couple of the largest towels she could find and then, as an afterthought, rifled through another section to find a pair of oversized painting overalls. He could get out of his jeans and wear these while his clothes dried.

Unable to stop the image of his bare legs invading her thoughts, she flushed, and hoped her cheeks wouldn't betray her.

She walked slowly down the stairs, and after taking a steadying breath re-entered the porch.

"I found a pair of painting overalls. You can get out of your wet clothes and throw them into the dryer," she said coolly. "There's a washroom just inside this door, next to the laundry room. If you want, I can pat down your dog."

She handed him the overalls and one of the towels.

He reached out for them and the towel fell open. His eyebrows rose and he glanced at her with a quirky half-smile. "I like the color, but I'm afraid they're a tad too small for me. But thanks."

Justine wanted the floor to split open and swallow her up. She snatched the hot pink bikini panties from where they clung to the towel and shoved them in her pocket. They must have been in the dryer together. She bent down to dry Luna, not wanting Casson to see how mortified she felt.

She let out her breath when she heard him enter the house.

Luna whimpered at the next rumble of thunder and started skittering around the porch. "Come here, Luna, you big scaredy-cat," she said. "Come on." To her surprise the dog gave a short bark and came to her, tail wagging. "Good dog. Now, lie down so I can dry you."

Luna obeyed, and Justine patted her head and dark coat with the towel. She was a mixed breed—Labrador Retriever, for sure, and maybe some German Shepherd. Her doleful eyes and the coloring around the face and head—tan and white, with a black peak in the middle of her forehead—made Justine wonder if there were some beagle ancestry as well.

"Don't you have pretty eyes?" she murmured,

chuckling as Luna rewarded her with a lick on the hand.

They looked as if someone had taken eyeliner to them. And the brown of her coat tapered off to tan before ending in white paws, making it seem as if she had dipped them in white paint.

"You're such a pretty girl—you know that?" Justine gave her a final patting and set down the towel. "Even if you've left your fur all over my towel."

Justine crouched forward and scratched behind Luna's ears. Before Justine could stop her Luna had sprung forward to lick her on the cheek. Unprepared for the considerable weight of the furry bundle, Justine lost her balance and fell back awkwardly on the floor.

"Luna, come!"

Casson's voice was firm, displeased. She hadn't heard him come back.

"It's all right, she was just being affectionate," Justine hurried to explain. "I lost my footing."

She scrambled to get up, and her embarrassment dissipated when she saw him standing there in a T-shirt and the white overalls. It wasn't the T-shirt that made her want to burst out laughing. Under different circumstances those muscled arms would certainly have elicited emotions other than laughter. It was the overalls—the not-so-oversized overalls.

They fit him snugly, and only came down to just above his ankles. How could someone so ruggedly handsome look so…so *dorky* at the same time? She covered her mouth with her hand, but couldn't help her shoulders from quaking as she laughed silently. Here was Mr. Perfect—the stylish, wealthy entrepreneur Casson Forrester—wearing something that looked like it belonged to Mr. Bean.

Casson's eyes glinted. "What? You find this fashion statement humorous? Hmm… I suppose it does detract from your previous impression of me, however—"

The boom of thunder drowned out his words, and as the rain pelted down even harder Justine motioned toward the door. Once they were inside she ran to make sure all the windows were closed. The rain lashed against the panes, obliterating any view at all. She turned on a lamp in the living room.

"Have a seat." She gestured toward the couch.

"I need to check the windows upstairs and change my clothes too." She glanced at Luna, who was whimpering. "You might want to turn on the TV to drown out the thunder."

After Justine had left, Casson smirked at the memory of her face when she'd turned to find him and Luna inside her porch. Her eyes had almost doubled in size, with blinking lashes that had reminded him of delicate hummingbird wings. Peach lips had fallen open and then immediately pursed. It had taken him everything not to burst out laughing.

Although laughing was not what he'd wanted to do when her pink panties had emerged from that towel… Her cheeks had immediately turned almost the same intense color, and he'd felt glad he hadn't given in to the impulse to hand them to her.

It had been her turn to smirk, though, when he'd appeared in these painting overalls. Casson knew he looked ridiculous—but, given the situation, beggars couldn't be choosers.

He grabbed the remote and found a classical music channel that would diffuse some of the thunder noise. Sitting back on the couch, he looked around with interest. The stone fireplace across from him was the focal point of the room, with its rustic slab of oak as mantel, and the Parry Sound stone continued upward to the pine-lined cathedral ceiling.

He drew a quick intake of breath as his gaze fell on the Group of Seven print above the mantel. *Mirror Lake*, by Franklin Carmichael. His eyes followed the curves of the multi-colored hills, the bands of varying hues of red, blue, purple, turquoise, green and gold and the perfect stillness of the lake, its surface a gleaming mirror.

This piece always tugged at his emotions and brought back so many memories—memories he didn't want to conjure up right now, with Justine set to return at any moment.

Casson's gaze shifted to the oversized recliners flanking the fireplace, one with a matching ottoman. Their colors, along with the couch and love seat, were an assortment of burnt sienna, brown and sage-green, with contrasting cushions. The wide-plank maple flooring, enhanced by a large forest green rug with a border of pine cones and branches, gave the place an authentic cottage feel, and the rustic coffee table and end tables complemented the décor.

The far wall behind the love seat featured huge windows of varying sizes, the top ones arching toward the peak of the ceiling and the largest one in the middle a huge bay window, providing what must be a spectacular view of the bay when the rain wasn't pounding against the panes.

A well-stocked bookshelf against one wall, eclectic lighting, and a vase containing a mix of wildflowers enhanced what Casson considered to be the ideal Georgian Bay cottage. He sat back, nodding, making mental notes for his future resort cottages.

After making a few investigative circles around the room Luna plunked down at his feet, panting slightly, her ears perked, as if she were expecting the next clap of thunder. Casson leaned forward to give her a reassuring pat and she grumbled contentedly and settled into a more relaxed position.

Casson wished *he* could feel more relaxed, but the painting overalls were compressing him in too many places. He wondered what Miss *Wintry*'s reaction would be if he stretched out on the couch. At least then he wouldn't feel like his masculinity was being compromised, he thought wryly. He checked the time on his watch. Sighing, he lay back and rested his head on one cushion.

Ah, relief.

He closed his eyes and listened to the classical music, accompanied by the rain pelting against the windows. A picture of Justine changing into dry clothes popped into his head.

Would she be slipping on those pink panties?

What was he doing?

He was here to wait for his clothes to dry and the storm to pass, not to imagine her naked…

Upstairs in her room, Justine peeled off her clothes, dried herself vigorously, and wished she could jump into a hot shower. But that would have to wait until Casson was gone. She didn't want to be thinking about him while she was… undressed. She changed quickly into white leggings and a long, brightly flowered shirt.

As an afterthought she opened her closet and moved a few boxes until she found the one she was looking for. Although Christmas was months away, she stashed away presents whenever she could instead of waiting for the last minute. The box she opened contained a dressing robe she had picked out for her dad. It was forest green, with burgundy trim at the wrists and collar, and she had embroidered the letters 'WH', for Winter's Haven, on one side. She had wanted to surprise her dad with this as a new idea—providing a robe in each cottage, like they did in hotels.

She lifted it out of the box and its tissue wrapping and hooked it over her arm. At the door she hesitated, feeling a sudden twinge of guilt, and then, before she could change her mind, she strode downstairs.

The TV was on and Luna was lying at Casson's feet. Justine held out the robe. "I thought you might appreciate this instead," she said.

He stood up and took it from her, before tossing the cushion he was holding back on the couch. "Indeed I do," he said, his jaw twitching. "Now I know you're not all flint and arrows."

Justine opened her mouth to voice a retort but his hand came up.

"No offence intended," he said. "I realize we didn't start off on exactly a positive note but, given the present circumstances, could we perhaps call a truce of some sort?"

Justine was taken aback. "We're not in a battle, Mr. Forrester. So there's no need for a truce. Excuse me. I'm going to put on some fresh coffee. Care for a cup?" She turned toward the open-concept kitchen/dining room.

"Love some coffee," he replied. "Just milk or cream, no sugar. And you'll have to excuse *me* as well. I'm dying to get out of these overalls."

He smirked and headed toward the washroom. Luna lifted her head quizzically, gave a contented grumble, and promptly settled back into her nap.

When Casson came back into the living room he had the overalls neatly folded. He placed them on a side chair and then sat down on the couch. The robe fit him well, which meant it would have been a size or two too big for her dad.

"That coffee smells great," he drawled, tightening the sash on the robe before crossing his legs.

Justine came out of the kitchen with a tray holding two mugs, a small container of cream and a plate of muffins. She caught her breath at seeing him there, one leg partially exposed. She felt a warm rush infuse her body. It was such an *intimate* scenario: Casson leaning back against the couch, totally relaxed, as if he were the owner of the place.

She saw his gaze flicker over her body as she approached. She wanted to squirm. Her jaw tensed. This was *her* place. Why did she suddenly feel like she was at a disadvantage?

She would *not* let him know that his presence was affecting her. She would treat him like any other cottage guest. Politely, respectfully. And hopefully the heavens would soon clam up and she could send him on his way. His clothes shouldn't take too long to dry.

She set the tray down on the coffee table and, picking up the plate of four muffins, held it out to him. "Banana yogurt. Homemade."

"Thank you, Miss Winter."

He reached forward and took one. At the same time Luna lifted her head, sniffing excitedly. Before Justine had a chance to move the plate Luna had a muffin in her jaws. Startled, Justine tipped the plate and stumbled over Casson's foot. She felt herself falling backward, and a moment later landed in the last place she'd ever want to land. A steaming volcano would have been preferable.

She felt his arms closing around her. The muffin was still in his hand.

"Now that you've fallen right into my lap," he murmured huskily in her right ear, "would you like to share my muffin?"

CHAPTER THREE

JUSTINE COULD FEEL Casson's breath on the side of her neck. She shivered involuntarily. His left arm was around her waist and his right arm was elevated, holding the muffin. His robe had opened slightly in the commotion and, glancing downward, she saw to her consternation that one bare leg was under her.

She was sitting on his bare leg.

Her head snapped up. She was glad he couldn't see her face. She needed to get off him. But to do so would mean pushing down against him to get some leverage. She bit her lip. Why didn't he just give her a push? That would avoid her needing to grind into him.

She cleared her throat. Luna had downed one muffin and was eyeing the two that had flipped onto the coffee table.

"Oh, no, you don't." Casson's voice was firm. "Luna, lie down."

His tone brooked no argument. With a doleful look at the muffins, and then at her master, Luna obeyed with a mournful growl. And then Casson gave Justine a gentle push and she was out of his lap.

He set down his muffin and crouched down to face Luna. "Dogs don't eat muffins," he said emphatically, before giving Luna a low growl.

Justine knew that Casson was emphasizing his alpha male status. Luna responded with a look of shame at being reprimanded, and Justine couldn't help chuckling—which caused Luna to begin wagging her tail, her doggy enthusiasm restored.

Casson lifted an eyebrow and Justine wondered if he was going to growl at *her* for interrupting his disciplinary moment. She saw his mouth twitch and he rose, grabbed his mug and muffin and sat down again.

"And no whining!" he reproached Luna, who flopped back on her side.

Flustered, and trying not to show it, Justine sat down on the love seat. She sipped her coffee and turned to glance out the big bay window. Through the sheets of rain battering the pane she could glimpse patches of sky and bloated gray-black clouds. The water in the bay would be churning, the whitecaps foaming.

"Good muffin." Casson reached for the two still on the coffee table and handed one to her. "I hope these are for sale in the diner."

Justine took it from him and broke off a piece from the top. He seemed totally comfortable sitting in her living room, lounging with nothing on but a robe. She concentrated on pulling the paper back from the muffin and forced herself to avoid glancing at his well-muscled calves and bare feet. And the slight patch of hair in the V below his neck.

She hoped the rain would abate soon. She nibbled at her muffin and took long sips of her coffee, and then realized she hadn't responded.

"Um…yes, we do have muffins for sale in the diner. I usually make a fresh batch every morning…"

The thought of being alone with Casson for much longer was disturbing—mostly because her body was betraying her physically, reacting in a way that was not in sync with her mental perception of Casson Forrester. Her mind had reacted coolly to him from his first arrogant appearance;

however, her body was becoming increasingly warm…in ways that made her want to squirm.

"What made you want to return here?" Casson asked with a note of genuine curiosity.

Justine looked up from her muffin and stared blankly at him, her mind scrambling to come up with an alternative explanation, since she had no intention of revealing the truth to him. Her involvement with Robert was none of Casson's business.

"It really doesn't matter," she said, making her voice light. "I'm just glad I returned when I did… to save our humble property from certain demise." She finished her muffin and folded the paper muffin cup several times, before setting it down on the table. "But I'm willing to forget our first negative meeting if you are. We might as well be civil to each other, since you own the Russell properties now."

She picked up her mug and sipped while gazing at him, wondering how he would reply.

Casson stood up and walked to the bay window. He drank his coffee and stared out at the storm. Justine wondered if he intended to ignore her peace offering. Her heart thudded against her chest as she watched him, standing there in the robe. The dark green suited him. His hair was thick, and slightly longer than when she had first seen him, and his short beard did not detract from his good looks. In fact, she was having a hard time deciding if he was more handsome with or without it.

Casson turned then and she started, realizing how intently she had been staring at him.

"Of course we can be civil."

He eyed her for a moment, then left his position at the window to sit down next to her on the love seat. Justine drummed a quiet beat on the arm of the seat, wondering why his eyes were glittering so devilishly. Was the room getting darker, or was it just her imagination?

What they needed was more illumination, she decided, and was about to turn on the other table lamp when a deafening series of thunderclaps shattered her thoughts. Instinctively she swiveled toward Casson, both palms landing flat against his chest. Luna yelped and scampered around the room, barking and panting.

Casson clasped her shoulders. Simultaneously horrified and shocked at her reaction—and his—

she stared at him wordlessly, unable to wrench herself away. The rise and fall of his chest as he breathed made her shiver. While his eyes remained fixed on hers, his arms slid around to encircle her back.

Casson's face was suddenly closer, his eyes intense, and Justine felt herself quiver. His lips made contact with hers and involuntarily she closed her eyes. His arms tightened around her and his kiss deepened. Justine felt her lips open as if they had a mind of their own. His gentle exploration ignited sparks of desire along her nerve-endings.

As if he could sense her powerlessness to tear herself away, Casson guided her hands from his chest to the back of his neck. He pressed Justine tightly to him. She responded hungrily, caught in the moment. When she felt the intensity of his kiss diminish she opened her eyes. He pulled slightly away from her, his eyes searing hers, and with a muffled groan lowered his face to nuzzle her neck.

Justine froze, her pulse pounding as erratically as the raindrops beating relentlessly against the window panes. *What were they doing?* How could she have allowed her emotions to get out of control like that? She didn't even *like* this man, nor what he intended to do with his properties, and yet here she was, allowing him to be so *intimate* with her—as if they were a *couple.*

Casson must have felt her stiffening. He straightened and let her arms fall from around his neck. "That was a mistake," she said as steadily as she could, avoiding his gaze. "You'd better go."

She shifted away from him and crossed her arms and legs.

"Don't you want to know what I had to tell you?"

Justine looked at him in bewilderment, and then recalled his earlier words.

"After checking in on my store, I was about to officially start my holidays and head out to Winter's Haven when I spotted you in the paneling department."

Justine frowned. "Why *were* you heading out to Winter's Haven?" She looked at him pointedly. "You didn't actually think there was a chance that I'd change my mind about selling, did you? I told you before—I'm not interested in any proposal you have to make."

Casson's mouth lifted at one corner. "Perhaps you'll change your mind before my stay here is over," he said calmly, stroking his beard.

"That will never happen, believe—" She broke off, her eyes narrowing warily. "What do you mean, your stay *here*?"

"I plan to spend a week of my holiday at Winter's Haven. I'd like to see first-hand how things are run here."

"That's impossible." She gave him a frosty smile. "All twelve cottages are booked to the end of the summer."

Casson stood up lithely. "Just wait here a minute. I'll go check my clothes."

Justine watched him leave the room. Luna bolted after him and he turned, caught Justine's eye, and said, "Go back, Luna. Go lie down."

He winked at Justine and left the room.

Luna padded back and plunked herself down by Justine's feet. Despite her annoyance with Casson, Justine couldn't help being charmed by his big, friendly, generally well-behaved dog.

"Did you enjoy my muffin, you big cutie?" She laughed, patting Luna on the head, and Luna responded with a noisy yawn and rolled to one side. "Oh, now you want a belly rub, do you?" She smiled, leaning forward. "It's obvious your master spoils you."

"She deserves spoiling."

Casson's voice was behind her.

"Her original owner wasn't so nice to her. He left her on the side of the road and took off. Before I could drive up to the spot she was gone. I found her wandering in the woods. Fur all covered with burrs. She was barely a year old."

"Oh…poor baby."

Justine felt tears stinging her eyes. She blinked rapidly, but a few slipped down. Luna sat up and immediately licked her on the cheek.

Not wanting Casson to know how emotional she felt, Justine laughed and said, "Well, maybe I might just give you another muffin, Miss Luna."

"You'd better not," Casson advised. "Muffins are *not* part of her diet."

He stood across from her. He had changed back into his jeans and T-shirt, but his jacket was in his hands. He flung it on the arm of the couch and then reached into the pocket of his jeans. He held out a key that looked all too familiar to Justine.

She blinked. "Where did you get that?" she demanded. She could see the number engraved on it. The number one. For Cottage Number One—the cottage closest to her house. Justine stood up and reached for it. Casson's reaction was quick. He drew back his arm, leaving Justine grasping at thin air.

"How did you get that key? The Elliots are renting that cottage."

"They *were*," he corrected.

"But—"

"Let me explain," he interjected smoothly. "While I was waiting in the restaurant for you a couple of weeks ago I met the Elliots. Talking to them gave me the idea of renting one of your cottages. I made them an offer they couldn't refuse—an all-expenses-paid round-trip anywhere in the world in exchange for their cottage for a week." He smiled. "My timing was perfect. They had recently received an invitation from friends in Greece and declined, since they couldn't afford it. Needless to say, they jumped at my offer."

Justine gaped at him. "I can't *believe* this. They would have said something to me about it. It's against the rules to let someone else stay in their cottage without asking me or Mandy first. And *I* make the final decision."

Another infuriatingly smug smile. "I made them promise not to say anything. I told them I wanted to surprise my *very good friend* with a visit…and a *proposal*."

Justine's stomach muscles tightened. Her anger had been growing with his every word, and at this revelation she exploded. "A *proposal*? You had them believe you were going to *propose* to me?" She glared at him, her hands on her hips. "You had it all planned, didn't you? How dare you manipulate my customers to get what you want? You had no right to use the Elliots that way, for your own advantage."

"Would you have rented out a cottage to me if I had consulted you first?"

His voice was calm, which infuriated her all the more.

"Certainly not! I don't rent out to devious, untrustworthy, manipulative… Oh, what's the use?" She threw her hands up in the air. "You can't teach an old dog new tricks."

Casson chuckled. "I've been called many things by women—mostly positive, I might add—but 'old dog' is a new one for me." His eyes blazed down at her. "Could you be more specific as to the breed?"

"Don't try to be funny, Mr. Forrester, and make light of this. I'm not amused." She stuck out her hand. "The only decent thing for you to do is to give me back the key. Besides, you now own the properties on either side of me. Why don't you stay on one of *them* to carry out your surveillance tactics?"

"You make me sound like a spy," he countered wryly. "I admit you have a good point, Miss Winter, but although I now *own* the properties I can't really observe the way things are run at Winter's Haven unless I'm actually *here*. Day and night. I thought it fair to at least tell you before settling in."

"Fair?" She filled her lungs with air and let it out in a rush.

"Look, all I want is a week to see how this place operates." His eyes narrowed speculatively. "You never know—the experience might even change my mind about going ahead with a large-scale venture. I may find that a smaller operation is more in keeping with the balance of nature in this area…"

"I have no guarantee that you will change your mind," Justine retorted, "and I refuse to be subjected to your scrutiny for any length of time. Your tactics are futile. I have no intentions of selling to you. *Ever.* Now, give me the key, please. My hand is getting tired." She glowered at him. "What you did may have negative legal implications—which, I assure you, I will look into if you do not return my key."

"There's nothing illegal about what I did and you know it," he said, putting the key back in his jeans pocket. He glanced out the bay window. "I see the rain has stopped for the time being so, if you'll excuse me, I'd like to take advantage of your dining facilities…"

He turned to leave.

"Won't you join me, Miss Winter?"

Justine was sure her face was aflame. "No, thank you," she replied icily, her blue-gray eyes flashing a warning at him. He was pushing her too far. If he didn't soon leave she would throw… throw the remaining muffin or a cushion at him.

"See you later then," he said with a slight nod.

"Come on, Luna, I'll take you to your new digs. I don't believe you're allowed in the diner." When he opened the door to the porch, he called out, "Thank you for taking us in. Luna and I enjoyed the muffins…and your company."

Justine swiveled around with a retort on the tip of her tongue, but he was already out the door. Deflated, she sank back down on the love seat.

Casson felt like letting out a boyish cheer as he left Justine's place. *Step one, accomplished!* The rain had diminished to a soft drizzle, which he barely noticed as he opened the side door of his pickup truck. Luna jumped in happily, turning several times in her spot until sinking down, her big brown eyes looking at him expectantly.

Casson grinned and gave her several pats on her rump. "I suppose I should thank you for your part in this, Luna Lu."

Luna gave a soft bark. Casson laughed and reached into his pocket.

"I may not have Miss Winter in the palm of my hand, but it sure felt good having her in my lap."

And tasting her lips.

It was the last thing he'd expected to happen between them. He hadn't planned it, but he couldn't say he regretted it. How could he regret the feel of those soft, pliant lips against his? The way they'd opened to him, let him in deeper? The feel of her under that thin T-shirt, pressed against him so tightly? A mistake, she'd called it. But he had felt the electricity between them as she withdrew.

He wondered if she suspected he was using his masculine wiles to influence her and weaken her resolve about refusing to sell. That was not his intention, but he doubted she would believe him if he attempted to explain. So of course he had feigned indifference at her withdrawal, and proceeded to explain why he wanted to stay at Winter's Haven.

He drove back to the Russell house—*his* house now—and set down his briefcase on the kitchen table. He pulled out a thick folder containing the deeds to his new properties. Now that he was actually on the main property he wanted to examine the maps and surveyors' documents again. He wanted to become familiar with every curve, corner and contour of his land and shoreline.

Even on paper, the Russell and Winter properties occupied an impressive stretch of the Georgian Bay shoreline. The Russells had cleared very little of this property—just enough to snake a path through the dense forest and construct their home on the main parcel and a small cottage on the second one.

Casson peered closely at the map showing the zoning of the adjoining properties. He examined the boundaries of Winter's Haven. It was obvious the Winters had also endeavored to maintain the rugged features of their property. Even though they had eventually added twelve cottages to the land, and an office/diner, they, too, were built with minimal clearing and, like the Russell property, sat further back from the shoreline.

Casson stared at one of the more detailed zoning maps. He shuffled through the folder and pulled out an older document. He rubbed his jaw thoughtfully as he compared them. He was no zoning expert, but he was certain there was a discrepancy in the documents. The older one showed the adjoining properties before any structures had been built. The document showing the addition of the properties revealed something that made him start.

Why hadn't this been brought to his attention? Had the realtor even been aware of it?

Casson knew that both structures had been built in the fifties, and evidently had been beautifully maintained, with occasional renovations, but one thing he hadn't known was the way a section of the Winter home had been erected on a slice of land that clearly belonged to the Russells.

Casson let out a deep breath. Justine's place was sitting partially on *his* property.

He was certain she had absolutely no knowledge of this. Her parents probably didn't either. Or if they did they hadn't revealed it to Justine. It might have been an oversight that the Russells had dismissed, given that they owned so much land. *And* they had been the best of friends with the Winters. Mr. Winter had said as much, when he and Casson had first discussed the potential sale of Winter's Haven.

Casson drummed his fingers on the smooth surface of the table. He wasn't sure he wanted to share his findings with his new neighbor. Not just yet. But he would write a letter to Justine and wait for the appropriate time to give it to her.

He pulled out his laptop and quickly typed it

up, ending with an invitation to meet him and discuss options. He was glad he had brought his portable printer with him—a habit, since he did so much travelling. After printing out a copy, he placed the letter and the other documents in an envelope and into his briefcase, along with his laptop.

Casson looked around. There would be time enough to enjoy his new place after a week at Winter's Haven.

With a feeling of anticipation for the week ahead, Casson grabbed his briefcase and the one piece of luggage that he had packed the night before. Heading out to his truck with Luna, he began to whistle.

He couldn't wait to settle in to Cottage Number One.

CHAPTER FOUR

NONE OF THE cottagers were in the diner yet. Justine glanced at the board indicating the special of the day—turkey cranberry burgers with arugula salad—and helped herself to a cup of coffee before sitting at one of the tables by the window. Mandy was still in the office, on the phone with a booking. Justine had waited for a bit, anxious to tell her what Casson Forrester had had the nerve to do, but Mandy had waved her away, indicating she would join her when she was done.

Justine sipped her coffee and looked out at the bay. The sky was a slate of gray, ruffled with layers of low cloud. She thought about Casson Forrester settling in to Cottage Number One and felt a shiver run through her body.

She replayed earlier events in her mind—from her realization that the jerk following her was Casson, to his barging into her home with Luna and the deafening series of thunderclaps that had caused her to end up in Casson's arms. The last thing she had ever imagined when he'd first strode into the office was that she'd be thoroughly kissed by him in her own home…*and that she'd thoroughly enjoy it.*

She wasn't sure how long she had sat frozen on the love seat after Casson had left. She'd felt like she had been tossed about in a whirlwind, and had had to let her brain and body restore its calm and balance. Her feelings had alternated between fury at being manipulated and helplessness. She'd pondered calling a local police officer she knew, who had breakfast regularly in the diner. But what could he do, really? Perhaps she needed to consult a lawyer to see if there was a way of getting Casson Forrester off her property…

Do you really want him off your property?

Justine started at the tiny inner voice that had popped into her mind. To be honest with herself, if Casson had been renting a cottage for a week or more, without any intention to take over, she would have been happy—*thrilled* would be more accurate. After all, who *wouldn't* want to have the pleasure of looking at such a fine specimen of a man for any length of time? Despite the fact that she had been duped by Robert, she wasn't so jaded that she could ignore the presence of someone as handsome as Casson.

But the fact of the matter was that Casson had an ulterior motive in staying at Winter's Haven. And even if he *had* kissed her it was her property he wanted, not *her.*

"Hey, Justine. What are you dreaming about?" Mandy smiled and sat down across from her.

Justine snapped out of her thoughts and took a deep breath. "Remember Casson Forrester, who was here last week?"

Mandy's eyes widened. "Mr. Gorgeous, you mean? The hunk I wish they'd name an ice cream flavor after?"

"Mandy! You're *engaged*, remember?" Justine couldn't help laughing.

"I'm engaged—not blind!"

"Well, Mr. Forrester has just finagled his way into staying at Winter's Haven. He wants to observe how things are run up close. I guess he figures he'll find a way to convince me to sell. He's staying in Cottage Number One for a week."

Justine paused, watching Mandy's face wrinkle in confusion. She clearly had no idea of the transaction between Casson and the Elliots.

"*What?* How can that be? The Elliots are in there!"

Justine explained, then sat back, crossing her arms. "Now, what should we do? Call Constable Phil? A lawyer?"

"Geez…" Mandy's brows furrowed. "Do we want to complicate things? Other than being hot, Casson Forrester seems pretty harmless. Ambitious, maybe, but not dangerous. Look, you're not going to sell, so why don't you just let him enjoy the cottage and in a week's time you can kiss him goodbye!"

Justine knew Mandy was speaking figuratively, but the thought of kissing Casson again gave her a rush. She felt her cheeks burn, and saw Mandy looking at her speculatively, but she wasn't ready to share what had happened…

"I hate to spring another surprise on you, Justine, but the call I just took…" Mandy sighed. "It was *Robert*. He wants to see you. He tried to book a cottage."

Justine just about dropped her coffee mug. She set it down and stared at Mandy. "What for?"

Mandy took a deep breath. "He told me that he knows he made mistakes but that he hopes you'll give him a chance to apologize."

"He's the *last* person I want to see," Justine moaned, covering her face with her hands.

"I hope you're not talking about *me,* Miss Winter."

Justine slowly let her hands slip from her face.

"And I hope you don't mind if I join you for lunch." Casson looked at her directly. "I haven't picked up any supplies for my stay yet, and I hear the locals come to eat here a lot, which convinces me I should try it." He glanced over at Mandy. "Hello, Miss Holliday. Nice to see you again." He offered his hand.

"My pleasure." Mandy beamed. "And, yes—please join us."

Justine wanted to scowl at her, but Casson had turned to look at her again.

"Only if the Boss Lady agrees," he said, amusement tinging his voice.

"That's fine," Justine said, trying to keep from clenching her teeth.

Casson pulled out a chair to sit next to Mandy.

"Actually, I'm not staying for lunch," Mandy

said. "My fiancé's taking me out." She waved at Justine and Casson. "See you later."

She glanced slyly at Justine, and Justine shot her a *Just wait 'till you get back* glare.

When a waitress walked over and set down two glasses of water for them Casson thanked her and looked over at Justine expectantly.

Justine flushed. "Hi, Mel. Casson Forrester—meet Melody Green, our wonderful waitress."

After Melody had taken their orders—turkey burger for her and fish and chips for him—Casson flashed Justine a smile. "I can see why people want to stay at Winter's Haven," he smiled. "The cottage is perfect. Luna has already found her favorite spot." As Justine's eyebrows went up, he said, "Couch in the living room. She's curled up on it right now." He chuckled. "But I don't doubt she'll find a way to join me on the bed tonight."

Casson saw something flicker in Justine's eyes. He might be totally out in left field, but was that a spark of—?

"She's a nice dog," Justine said grudgingly.

"And she's very protective of her owner." Casson grinned.

"I can't imagine *you'd* need protecting."

Casson gave a hearty laugh. "I might—if the owner of this place becomes aggressive with me." He gazed quizzically at Justine. "But, then again, Luna likes you. If you tried to tackle me she'd probably do nothing. Or think we were playing and try to join in." He gazed at her for a few seconds.

Justine's face wrinkled into a frown. "There would be no reason for me to tackle you, Mr. Forrester."

"*Please*. Call me Casson. After all, we'll be neighbors for the next week. By the way—I have a couple of guests coming to spend the weekend with me. I figured it was okay, since the cottage has a loft and a pull-out couch. But I did want to mention it in case there's an extra charge."

He looked expectantly at Justine. She was slightly taken aback, judging by her hesitation in responding and the sudden tapping of her foot against the table leg, which she seemed unaware of.

"Yes, a limited number of guests are allowed. There is a minimal charge."

"Great—just add it to my bill." Casson nodded in satisfaction.

"Here are your orders," Melody announced cheerfully. "Enjoy." She placed a platter in front of each of them. "Is there anything else you'd like to drink, Mr. Forrester?"

"Water will be fine, thanks." He slipped her a couple of bills. "No change needed." He smiled at Melody's look of appreciation, and then picked up one of his fries. *"Bon appétit."* He winked at Justine.

They ate silently for a couple of minutes, and even though Casson tried not to make it obvious he couldn't help glancing occasionally at Justine. While he enjoyed his fresh-cut fries and battered whitefish, Justine was trying to eat a massive burger delicately. When she set her bun down in frustration he saw a smear of ketchup on her cheek and chin. He had a crazy desire to lean over and lick it off her face.

But of course he wouldn't.

Casson watched as she ran her tongue over her lips and just outside her mouth. His heart did a flip. He picked up a clean napkin and, rising slightly, reached over and gently wiped at the two spots of ketchup, his eyes locking with hers.

It was like looking into the bay. *Deep blue. A blue that could swallow you up.*

He didn't know how long he stayed in that position, half out of his seat, but when he sat down he felt like something had knocked him out temporarily. Justine's face was flushed, and she immediately looked down and concentrated on finishing her burger.

"By the way, it seems that one of your prospective guests couldn't book a cottage here, so he asked around and was told about the Russell properties being under new ownership. He came looking for me and asked if he could rent the small cottage." Casson shrugged. "I hadn't even thought about renting it, but what the heck? Might as well let someone enjoy the place."

He saw Justine stiffen. "Who did you rent it out to?" Her voice trembled slightly.

"A lawyer called Robert Morrell."

CHAPTER FIVE

JUSTINE WANTED THE floor to open up and swallow her. It was bad enough that she had an issue with Casson. Having to deal with Robert now was just too much. She had spent the last couple of months convinced she was finished with him, and had never imagined he would come to see her here at Winter's Haven. Not knowing what he was planning to do jangled her nerves. She couldn't believe he had called the office and tried to rent a cottage… He could walk into the diner at any moment…

She realized Casson had asked her a question… asked if she knew Robert. "Yes, I know him." She tried to respond in a neutral tone, so Casson wouldn't ask any more questions, but she heard her voice crack.

She saw Casson looking at her thoughtfully. The sun had nudged its way through the clouds, shining through the window, and it was reflected in his deep brown eyes. His suntanned face with its dark beard, his plaid shirt with its rolled-up sleeves and his jeans made him look like a muscled hiking guide. She felt her heartbeat accelerating.

"Old boyfriend?"

Justine stared at him. "How did you—?"

"Know? You're not that hard to read. You know that expression '*wearing your heart on your sleeve*'? Well, with you, your feelings show on your face."

Justine cocked her head at him and frowned.

He nodded. "Yup. Eyelashes fluttering. Blue eyes darkening. Cheeks flushing. All the classic signs." His eyes narrowed and he leaned forward. "Did you dump *him* or was it the other way around?"

Justine wanted to squirm. Casson wasn't her *friend*, for goodness' sakes. She wasn't about to reveal anything about her past to him, and nor did she intend to enlighten him as to who had dumped whom.

While she grappled with an appropriate response Casson leaned back again and took a long drink of his water. Afterward he stood up, and with a nod said, “Sorry. I was being nosy. Nice doing lunch. I’ll see you later…” He turned away and then glanced back at her. “If he let you go, he was a fool…”

Not waiting for her to reply, he walked out of the diner.

Justine followed him with her eyes until the last inch of him was out of sight. Reaching for her handbag, she shuffled through it for her keys. She left the diner and got into her car. She was glad she had already planned to go into Parry Sound to pick up her order of bread for the diner. Now, with the disheartening news about Robert, she decided she’d stay away even longer.

Justine headed first to *West Lake Cosmetics.* She loved owner Wendy’s natural handmade soaps, skincare products and bath treats. She also stocked the cottages with products having names like *Muskoka Mimosa*, *Rose Rapture* and *Georgian Bay Linen*. After today’s stress, she needed *something* to help her relax.

She chose a *Rose Rapture* soap and a *Citrus Wave* bath pod, and looked forward to pampering herself later with a long, soothing bath. But first she'd have to relieve Mandy for the afternoon shift.

Justine left the shop and moments later stepped into *The Country Gourmet Café and Gallery* to pick up the loaves she had ordered for the diner and two walnut loaves for herself. She thanked Chris, the friendly owner, then headed back to Winter's Haven and tried not to think about Robert.

Everything looked fresh and clean after the earlier downpour. Justine rolled down her windows, lifted her face to the warm breeze and thought about Casson's last words. *If he let you go, he was a fool...* Her heart catapulted at the memory, just as it had done when he had uttered the words.

She replayed the conversation in her head as she drove, and wondered why Casson had wanted to know who was responsible for the ending of her relationship with Robert.

Robert!

He was the one who had decided to break things off. Unable to face working with him every day, Justine had resigned immediately and fled to Winter's Haven for a few days, needing the support of her parents. She had been stunned when they'd made her the offer…

She'd gone back to Toronto and fortunately had only had to wait a month for the end of the lease on her apartment. But it had been the hardest month to get through. She'd had lots of time to process the failed relationship. To go over every painful detail of how Robert had taken advantage of her trust, her naiveté. She winced at the memories, and a rash of anger ignited and spread under her skin.

She *had* been naïve. She had allowed Robert to draw her in, letting her care for him while his marriage deteriorated. Robert had used her, milking her genuine concern and thoughtfulness until she had been practically frothing over him. She had believed his intentions to be honorable, and his betrayal had hit her like a winter gale from Georgian Bay.

By the end of the month she'd accepted that it was over and had become determined not to allow anyone to use her again. She'd realized it was a godsend that her parents had offered her the opportunity of taking over the business.

It had been time to leave the city and go home.

When she'd driven into Winter's Haven two months ago, and breathed in the fresh scent of the woods and the bay, she'd known she had made the right decision. The chapter of her life with Robert Morrell in it was finished.

Until now.

Justine took a deep breath and let it out slowly. She dropped off the loaves to Melody, took over the office from Mandy, and tried to focus on business tasks. Every once in a while she looked up, wondering anxiously if Robert would suddenly appear.

Justine was relieved when the time came to close up the office. When she got home she kicked off her shoes, put away the bread, and eagerly reached for the bag inside her purse. She was more than ready for a relaxing Citrus Wave bath. And, although it was not yet eight, she started to fill up the tub. She began to undress—then heard the doorbell ring.

Her heart skipped a beat. Was Casson here with another strategy to entice her to sell? He *had* said, "I'll see you later…"

Justine slipped her T-shirt back on and flew

down the stairs to the front door. Through the window curtain she could make out a profile.

Wrong man.

When Casson entered his cottage he made a pot of coffee and satisfied himself that the place was ready for his guests' stay. His cousin Veronica would be arriving around noon the following day, along with her son Andy.

Casson smiled. Andy was such a good kid. When he was born, five years ago, Ronnie had asked Casson to be his godfather and he had been thrilled. Ronnie was like a sister to him—the sister he'd never had.

Casson's jaw tightened. She had separated from her husband Peter over a year ago. Peter had been unable to deal with the day-to-day challenges of his son's illness, and had found solace in the comforting arms of a woman who was "there" for him.

But Ronnie had rallied and Andy was now in his second year of his treatment. He had recently finished another round of maintenance chemotherapy, and when Ronnie had texted Casson with this news he had immediately invited them to spend a weekend with him at Winter's Haven. To his delight, Ronnie had called to accept.

Casson poured himself a big mug of coffee before going out to sit on the back deck. Watching the blue waves, he found his thoughts returning to Justine, and the alarm he had glimpsed in her eyes when she'd found out Robert Morrell was renting his cottage.

His jaws clenched. Had the creep hurt her in some way?

He'd find an excuse to check on Robert tonight. And Justine, just to make sure she was okay. Whether it was his business or not, and despite the fact that he might very well be wrong in his suspicions, Casson needed to know what Robert Morrell wanted with Justine.

CHAPTER SIX

JUSTINE HESITATED. WHY had Robert waited until this evening to come and find her? She jumped as Robert tapped the door knocker. She could ignore him...but he probably would have seen her approaching through the lace curtain.

He knocked again. She bit her lip and opened the door slightly, the chain still in place. She didn't offer a greeting; she just gave him a cold stare.

"Justine... Look, I wouldn't blame you if you slammed the door in my face. I just... I just had to try to make things right with you." His voice had a slight tremor. "Even if we never see each other again."

Justine pursed her lips, unconvinced. She wasn't sure if he expected her to let him in, but she felt reluctant to let him step foot in her house. After all, she had never invited him to Winter's Haven before they'd split up—no, before he'd dumped her—so why should she allow him into her private space *now*?

And besides, did she really want to hear what he had to say?

Justine shivered, even though the evening air was warm and still.

She cleared her throat. "Why would you want to do that now, Robert?" She hoped her voice was cool, uncaring—unlike the way she had responded when he'd told her it was over.

Robert cringed visibly at her tone, as if she had just struck him across the face. "I want to apologize, Justine. Please—just let me try to make amends. I made a mistake in the way I treated you. You deserve more than an apology…"

He looked like a puppy dog, Justine thought, with doleful eyes that were begging for a little mercy. Justine felt herself waver. Robert sounded genuinely sorry. Maybe she needed to hear him explain his less than cavalier behavior toward her…

Nodding, she slid the door chain off. "I don't have a lot of time," she lied.

Relief flooded Robert's face. He stood hesitantly as Justine opened the door wider and then offered a grateful smile as he entered her home. He looked around appreciatively. "Nice place," he said, eyebrows lifting as his gaze settled on the bay window. "Beautiful view."

She gestured toward a recliner, away from the love seat…

Robert nodded and passed in front of her. And then she heard the water still flowing into the bathtub.

"Good heavens!" She threw him a panicked look. "I forgot to turn off the water."

She bolted up the stairs two at a time. She drew out a long breath of relief as she turned both taps off. The water level was an inch below the top of the tub. With jangled nerves she returned to the living room. She wanted to get this apology thing over with, see Robert out, and then have that relaxing bath she had planned.

She sat in the recliner opposite Robert and glanced at him pointedly.

He shifted in his seat, his forehead glistening with beads of perspiration. "Look, Justine, it was never my intention to hurt you. I—I was in a dark place emotionally with my wife, and you were like a ray of sunshine." He smiled at her crookedly. "Sorry, I know that's an overused cliché But after spending my evenings arguing with Katie, and my nights on a couch, I came to appreciate your positive, funny and charming personality… and I *wanted* that. I—I wanted *you.*"

He paused, waiting for her to reply, but she had nothing to say—*yet.*

"I was all mixed up. I admit it." He looked away and gazed at the view of the bay. "It was exciting to be with you, and yet once I'd tasted some freedom I started wanting even more. More freedom, more fun, more adventure."

Justine felt a jab in the pit of her stomach. "And that's when you decided to break up with me?" she said, as steadily as she could. "You said the whole divorce thing had depleted you and that you didn't have the energy to carry on with a serious relationship. Only I found out the *real* reason you were 'depleted' when I came to the office early the next morning to pack my things and leave my letter of resignation on your desk… That's when I spotted your lover's panty hose on the couch in your office."

He cringed again. "I'm sorry, Justine. I was screwed up. I know I crossed the line." He gazed at her helplessly. "I hope you can find it in your heart to forgive me. I was so mixed up. Afraid of another commitment but hungry for love. I played with fire and you were the one that got burned." His eyes glistened. "I was the loser, letting you go." His voice broke. "I'll do *anything* to have you back."

Justine let out a deep breath. She hadn't expected *this*.

"I've rented the cottage on the property next to yours for a few days, hoping I can eventually convince you to forgive me and give me another chance."

He stood up and began walking toward her. When he was a foot away, he got down on one knee.

"I—I'm not seeing that other woman, Justine. I swear it didn't mean anything." He placed a hand over hers. "Tell me what I can do to get you to come back to me."

Justine's heart began to hammer. But not because she was overcome with joy at Robert's words, she realized. And his touch left her cold. She tried to slide her hand out from under his but he tightened his grip. She frowned and, meeting his gaze, saw his dilated pupils. She caught the unmistakable smell of alcohol.

"Robert, please let go of my hand." She said it quietly, trying to keep the alarm out of her voice.

He swayed a bit and moved closer, ignoring her request. And then she saw it over his shoulder—the bottle cap he had left on the base of the fireplace.

He had brought a bottle with him.

She had never seen him in this state, and tried not to think about what might happen if he was not in his right mind. She had to think of something to get him out of her house.

"Look, Robert, I forgive you."

To her relief, he loosened his hold.

"You do?"

He gazed at her wonderingly, and Justine knew then that the alcohol he had consumed had started to take effect. While he still had that dazed expression Justine managed to get up and start ambling away from him. Her gaze fell on the bottle that peeked out of his back pocket.

"Yes, Robert." She gestured toward the door. "But now you need to get back to your cottage."

He scrambled to his feet. Justine bit her lip. His senses might be dulled, but otherwise—

"*Please* let me stay, Just—Justine."

In a flash, he had reached her, encircled her waist with both arms and was brushing his cheek against hers.

Justine inhaled the heavy scent of alcohol on his breath. Her stomach twisted, but before she could even think of breaking free he had pushed her back onto the couch and pinned her arms down. She tried to lift a knee but he flattened it with his own. She stared at his foggy eyes, and at the mouth that was looming over hers. She was strong, but he was a dead weight.

She closed her eyes, cringing at those lips about to touch hers…

"Luna—tackle!"

Sharp barks filled the room.

"Go get him!"

Robert Morrell backed away from Justine, only to be tackled by Luna. He was soon sprawled on the carpet, with Luna's paws and body over him, his face a mask of terror as she emitted low growls.

Casson strode over to help Justine up. Her eyes were wide as she took in the scene before her, her face blanched, her hair messed up. He gave her a tight hug, then with one hand swept her hair away from her face, something inside him melting as she met his gaze, her eyes glistening with relief and gratitude.

He turned away and, taking his phone out, proceeded to take several photos of Robert with Luna. "These are all I need to prove that you were trespassing." His jaw clenched. He shot an icy glare at Robert. "I hope you have a good lawyer. I'm calling the police."

"No, *pl-please*." Robert attempted to sit up, but promptly lay back as Luna growled and pushed her face into his. "I wasn't going to— Justine, I'm really sorry." Tears glazed his eyes. "I'll be ruined…" he moaned.

"You should have thought about the consequences of your actions," Casson ground out. "Luna—sit back."

In the pathetic state Robert was in, it was unlikely he would attempt anything. Luna obeyed, but stayed close to Robert, eyeing him warily.

Robert sat up, his head slumping in his hands. "Please…" He lifted his head and looked at Justine and then at Casson. "I promise I'll leave and never come back."

He had a resigned look in his eyes as his gaze

returned to Justine, and Casson caught Justine's ambivalent expression. He started to dial for the police, but she placed a hand on his arm.

It took everything he had to put his phone back in his pocket. His eyes bored into Robert's. "You're one lucky snake," he rasped. "I won't call the police, but if you ever try to come near Justine again I'll file charges immediately. Not only for trespassing, but for attempted sexual assault. And, trust me, I'm on the best of terms with Attorney Joseph Brandis." He saw Robert's eyes widen. "Yes, *the* Joseph Brandis."

He watched as Robert slowly got to his feet.

"I don't expect you to drive, in your condition, but I want you out of the cottage first thing in the morning. Give me your car keys. You can walk back; it'll clear your head. Tomorrow you can walk over to my place and get your car—understand?"

Robert nodded.

"I didn't hear you." Casson took a step toward him.

Robert flinched. "Yes, sir." He dug his keys out of his pocket and handed them to Casson.

"Luna, follow him out."

Luna gave a short bark and leapt up to obey.

Robert stopped at the door to look back at Justine. "I'm s-sorry." Shoulders slumped, he left, with Luna and Casson close behind.

Casson waited until Robert was out of sight. He gave a whistle and Luna came racing back, her tail wagging furiously. Casson crouched down and scratched behind her ears. "Good girl," he said, emotion catching in his voice. He reached in his pocket and gave her a treat before opening the door.

Justine was sitting down on the couch. Luna bounded toward her and nuzzled into her hands. She seemed to snap out of her stupor and leaned forward to caress her.

"Thank you, Luna Lu," she murmured.

Casson's heart constricted at her use of Luna's nickname. He watched Justine plant a kiss on Luna's forehead, then bury her face in the soft fur around Luna's neck. When he saw Justine's shoulders shaking, and Luna attempting to lick her cheeks, Casson realized Justine was crying.

In two strides he was crouched next to her and had her in his arms. He let her sob on his shoulder, her chest heaving against him.

"It's over," he said huskily, caressing the back of Justine's head. Then, slowly, his hand slipped to her cheek and he turned her face toward him. "You're safe now."

Justine's breath caught on a sob. "But what if you hadn't shown up with Luna?"

He took her chin in his hand and with his other hand stroked away her tears. "We showed up. That's all that counts."

He looked into her eyes, more gray than blue now. Her lashes were laced with teardrops, and he was overcome with a feeling of tenderness.

"Come and sit here," he murmured, leading her to the love seat. "I'll make you a hot drink."

He took the soft throw that was on the arm of the love seat and draped it around her shoulders. Luna jumped up beside her, but before he could reprimand her, Justine smiled weakly at him.

"Let her," she said. "I don't mind."

Casson strode to the kitchen. He needed a drink himself. Justine's words played over in his head. *What if you hadn't shown up with Luna?* He didn't want to think of what might have happened. If Robert had— No! He wasn't going there. It would just torment him. It was bad enough that he still had a picture in his mind of Robert bending over Justine, restraining her, about to put his mouth on hers.

Casson felt his stomach turn. He needed something stronger than milk. Brandy, maybe. He found a bottle, poured himself a shot, and put a lesser amount in Justine's milk.

"Okay, Luna—skedaddle." Casson sat next to Justine and handed her the cup of milk.

She took a tentative sip, then wrinkled her nose.

"Drink it all up," he ordered. "It'll help you sleep."

"Casson?" She looked at him with eyes that were starting to flutter in exhaustion. "Can you and Luna stay tonight?" She shuddered. "What if he comes back?"

Casson set down his glass, his heart jolting. He saw the fear in her eyes. "He won't come back," he assured her, squeezing her hand. "But, yes… we'll stay."

CHAPTER SEVEN

JUSTINE COULD BARELY keep her eyes open. She peered at Casson drowsily. “Thank you for staying. You can take the spare room…”

She stood up and headed for the stairs. Luna followed her with Casson close behind. At her doorway, she turned and pointed to the room across from hers. Casson nodded but didn’t move.

“Goodnight,” she murmured. “Oh, just a minute…”

She entered her room and grabbed the robe that hung behind her door. The one she had given him earlier.

Casson’s mouth lifted at one corner. “Thanks. Goodnight, Justine.” His hand brushed hers as he took the robe.

She saw something flicker in his eyes and wished she could tell him how much she yearned for his protective arms around her again, but she didn’t trust herself in the hazy state she was in. Inviting his embrace could only complicate things.

She needed to sleep. Put the traumatic encounter with Robert out of her mind. She'd have a clearer head in the morning, and maybe then she might be able to make sense of her feelings about Casson. *For* Casson.

She realized he was waiting for her to turn in before heading to his room.

"You might want to close your door, Justine, or you could find yourself sharing your bed tonight," he said huskily.

Justine felt something electric swirl inside her at the thought of him—

"With Luna."

Justine felt her cheeks burn. She lowered her gaze.

Of course. How ridiculous to think that he would—

"And then I would have to come in and get her off…"

Her head snapped up. There *was* something in his expression. She swayed suddenly and in a moment Casson was there, supporting her. She breathed in his pine scent, felt the strength of his bare arms. Her lips brushed against his neck, and she gasped when he suddenly scooped her up and carried her to her bed.

For timeless moments she felt she was suspended in paradise, with Casson's expression of concern spreading heat to every inch of her body. His eyes were fathomless, heady, and she wished the fog in her head would dissipate so she could—

"You've had a shock tonight, Justine. You need to sleep," he murmured against her ear as he set her down softly on top of the flowered quilt.

Luna nudged her way past him to place her head on the bed and he gave a soft chuckle.

"Don't even think about it, Luna Lu. You're sleeping with *me*, remember? Come on—let's go…"

Justine watched them disappear, and when she heard the click of the door she sighed and turned down the bedcovers. She undressed and slid into bed, too exhausted to find her nightie.

Within moments she felt herself drifting into sleep.

* * *

Leaving his door open a crack, Casson switched on a lamp on the night table and Luna settled down on the rug. He undressed and put on the robe, before stretching out on the bed.

He couldn't deny that Justine ignited something within him. Seeing her so vulnerable, unable to defend herself against Robert, had aroused something primeval in him. Maybe if Luna hadn't been there Casson might have given in to his baser instincts and pounded the guy. With no hesitation. But he had to admit he was glad that *that* scenario hadn't taken place. It wouldn't have been pretty.

Tonight had been an ordeal Justine wouldn't soon forget. He found himself wondering what exactly had happened in her relationship with Robert…how long they had been together… if she had enjoyed Robert's touch before their breakup…

Why did it bother him so much?

He hardly knew Justine. Yet when he had held her tight against him it had felt…*timeless.* Things had shifted, whether he liked it or not. She had managed to throw him off course. Made him question his motives. He had to regroup and think of a strategy that would give them both what they wanted. Surely they could find common ground and come to a compromise?

Somehow he didn't think it would be as easy as it sounded.

Listening to the raindrops batting softly against the window, he closed his eyes—although he wasn't sure how much sleep he'd get tonight, listening in case Justine called out…

Justine was awakened by a moan, and then realized it was coming from *her.* For a moment she felt confused, not sure where she was. Her head throbbed. She opened her eyes and instinctively squinted at the clock radio on her night table. *Almost five a.m.* She must have been dreaming, but she had no recollection of any details—and then she remembered the events of the night before. How Robert had come to ask for forgiveness, and how he had lost control. She felt her stomach constrict at the memory of how helpless she had felt, and how Casson and Luna had arrived just in time…

Why had they come to her house anyway?

She had been too shaken even to formulate this question last night, let alone ask Casson.

A warm rush permeated her body as she recalled how he had hugged her so tightly, prepared her a hot drink, scooped her up so effortlessly when she'd felt her knees give out... She had felt as safe as if she were snuggled within a silky cocoon. Even the effects of the brandy hadn't stifled the desire that had overcome her while suspended within those muscled arms. Nor the stab of disappointment when he'd set her down and left moments later.

Don't be silly, she chided herself. What had she *expected* him to do? She didn't know much about Casson Forrester, but one thing she instinctively knew was that he wasn't the type to take advantage of someone in such a compromised state.

And, despite her disappointment that he hadn't gone any further, she was relieved that he hadn't. If Casson took her in his arms again—and she had no reason to believe that he would even do such a thing—she wanted to have all her senses functioning at an optimal level, not depressed by alcohol or trauma...or a headache like the one she was experiencing now. She needed to take something quickly, before it escalated into a migraine.

She slipped out of bed and padded to the door. She started to turn the handle and suddenly froze.

She was naked, and Casson was in the room across from hers.

She shivered and retraced her steps to get her nightie from the plush chair by her bed. She stepped out of her room, glanced toward the room where Casson was sleeping, and tiptoed to the washroom, cringing when she heard the maple floor creaking on the way.

She closed the bathroom door gently and her gaze fell on the tub, still full of water. So much for her plans for a relaxing bath… She was about to drain it, then decided against it. It was still too early to make so much noise.

She found the bottle of pills and took two with water. She needed to have this headache gone before heading into the office. It was still too early to stay up, though. She'd be a wreck if she didn't catch a few more hours of sleep. She paused for a moment.

What day is this? Relief flooded her. *Friday. Her day off this week.*

But what if Robert came back?

She froze, and then reminded herself that Casson was with her. He would make sure Robert didn't come near her…

As she stepped gingerly into the hallway she heard a snuffle and looked across to see Luna's nose edging the door open. Before Justine could even think of dashing into her room Luna had bounded toward her.

Casson soon appeared, his hair disheveled, his robe obviously thrown on without thinking. It was inside out and he had tied the sash loosely. Justine felt her gaze settle on his muscled chest, the fine line of hair swooping downwards, and then she started to shiver…and giggle.

Casson's brow creased. "Do I look that funny?" He looked down at his robe.

Justine shifted. "No, it's your dog; she's tickling my feet."

She tried to back away from Luna, who was intent on giving her feet and calves a thorough licking. And then she realized how skimpy her nightie was. It was barely mid-thigh, with spaghetti straps and an eyelet trim around the sweetheart neckline. It wasn't transparent, but the fine cotton draped over her breasts accentuated their peaks.

Mortified, she started to edge toward her room, all too aware of Casson's gaze. Luna began to follow her.

"Luna—*stay.* Are you okay, Justine?"

His husky tone made her quiver inside, and she prayed her legs wouldn't buckle under her again. Although Casson was trying not to make it obvious, his eyes were flickering over her body, from her neck and shoulders all the way down to her thighs and calves. And then back to her eyes.

It couldn't have taken more than a couple of seconds, but to Justine it had felt like an eternity.

"Oh… Other than a dull headache, I'm okay." She crossed her arms over her chest. *"Stop, Luna."*

The dog had inched forward to start licking her feet again. Her tone had no effect on Luna, but in a flash, Casson was striding toward them both.

"Luna—stop." His voice was deep, authoritative, and he didn't have to put a hand on his dog. Luna snapped to attention and immediately assumed a sitting position, her chocolate-colored eyes never wavering from her master.

"You have to show who's Alpha," he said in a soft tone to Justine, his tawny eyes blazing, and she felt like melting on the spot.

CHAPTER EIGHT

IF JUSTINE DIDN'T soon go into her room he didn't think he could continue to maintain his composure. Standing there in that…that kerchief-sized nightie, she had *no* idea how she was affecting him.

His heartbeat had accelerated with every shift of his gaze. It had started with her tousled hair, sleep-flushed face and the graceful curve of her neck, then revved up as it descended to the compact but curvy areas covered by her nightie. Areas that he could only imagine cupping, squeezing, *kissing.* And the sight of those shapely tanned legs, and the way Justine had wriggled them away from Luna's attempts to lick them, had almost done him in.

Casson had had several relationships—all short-term, since he was determined to focus on building his business—but none of them had caused him the inner commotion he was feeling right now. He practically vibrated with the prime-val impulse to gather his woman in his arms, lay her down and make her yield to him. *Willingly.*

But she was not his woman.

He felt a jab in his gut. He had to put a stop to this.

"I don't know about you, but I doubt I'll be able to fall back to sleep." He tried to keep his gaze fixed on her eyes and not her body. "How about I make some coffee?"

"Sure," she said lightly, letting her arms drop to her side. "I'll just have a quick shower."

She pivoted slightly and rushed into her room—but not before Casson had caught a glimpse of her bareness under the nightie. He let out a long, long breath and went to get dressed.

His mission was getting harder by the minute.

When Casson went downstairs, he turned on the light switch in the kitchen and put on the coffee maker. While the coffee was brewing he took Luna outside. It was still dusky, and the grass was wet. He scowled when he saw Robert's car. Robert would no doubt be sleeping for a while yet.

Out of the corner of his eye he saw Justine's turquoise retro-style bicycle. An idea popped into his head and he grinned. In less than a minute he had the bike and Luna in Robert's car and was on his way to giving the creep his early-morning wake-up call.

No point making Robert walk back to his place. No, *he* would take his car to him, and personally see Robert off his property. The bike-ride back to Justine's would take no time at all, and Luna would enjoy the run.

Justine towel-dried her hair and went downstairs. Casson was pouring coffee into two mugs. He looked up and smiled. Justine's pulse quickened. He looked so at home, standing behind the island…

"Let's take our coffee into the living room," he suggested. "We can catch the sun rise over the bay."

Justine's heart thrummed. The way he said it made it sound so *intimate.* She felt her cheeks burn as she started to follow him, and then, remembering Robert, walked tentatively toward the window and glanced out.

"He's gone," Casson said gruffly, "and he won't be back. I promise you."

Justine nodded, picked up her mug, and headed to the living room. She didn't need the details.

She started as Luna bounded in front of her and leapt onto the couch next to Casson. Seeing that he was about to order her off, Justine quickly said, "She's fine. She deserves special treatment after saving me last night."

She sat down on the love seat and bit her lip, the memory of Robert's face looming over hers making her stomach twinge.

Casson picked up his mug and strode to the fireplace. He stared at the painting while drinking his coffee. "I love this one," he murmured. *"Mirror Lake."*

"Oh? You're familiar with Franklin Carmichael's work?"

Casson smiled at her as if what she'd asked were amusing. "His and his buddy A. J.'s—and the rest of the Group of Seven."

Justine's eyes widened. "A. J. *Casson*," she said slowly. "So, what *is* the connection between your name and his?"

"My grandparents lived on the same street as the Cassons in north Toronto. They became friends. They loved his work, and by the time they passed away, they had quite a collection. My mother inherited it. She *loved* the Group of Seven. Casson and Carmichael were her favorites. And I inherited everything when she died."

Something flickered in his eyes and his brows furrowed. Justine wondered if it was sadness at his mother's passing, but she didn't have the courage to ask.

"Which is why," he said lightly, "she named me and my brother after them."

"Casson and Carmichael?"

"Yes and no. Casson and Franklin." He set down his mug on the mantel. He turned away to face the painting squarely. "Franklin was my little brother."

Justine caught the slight waver in Casson's voice. *Was*, he'd said. She felt her heart sinking.

"My father bought a limited edition print of *Mirror Lake* for my mom when Franklin was born. After he died they donated it to the Hospital for Sick Children in Toronto."

CHAPTER NINE

CASSON TOOK A deep breath and turned to face Justine. She had a stricken look, and her eyes had misted.

"I'm sorry," he said, returning to sit at one corner of the couch—the corner nearest the love seat where Justine was sitting. "It wasn't my intention to bring up my past." He set down his mug and glanced back at the painting. "It's just that that particular painting brings back so many memories."

And pain.

"Please, don't apologize," Justine said, her voice husky. "I'm very sorry for your loss. I—I can't even imagine..."

Casson felt a warm rush shoot through him as he met Justine's gaze. Her blue-gray eyes had cleared and were as luminous as the lake in the painting. He didn't make a habit of bringing up the death of his brother, but something in her expression made him willing to talk about it.

"It happened a long time ago," he said, patting Luna absentmindedly. "I was ten. Frankie was seven." He paused, his mind racing back to his childhood. "They found out he had a rare form of leukemia when he was six. He was rushed to SickKids and they started treatment immediately. Mom stayed with him there, and Dad stayed home with me."

Casson looked out beyond the bay window. The sky was beginning to lighten, with intersecting bands of pink and pale blue. His stomach contracted at the memories of that year: his father becoming increasingly moody and agitated; the empty house when he got home from school; no welcoming hug and snacks from his mother; no little brother to play hockey or baseball with; his bad dreams and the nagging worry that Franklin would die…

"That must have been so tough…"

Casson's gaze shifted back to Justine. He breathed deeply. "What was really tough was visiting him at SickKids. Seeing him with no hair, covered with bruises. Seeing him attached to tubes and hooked up to machines." His jaw clenched. "He was so small." Casson shook his head and averted his gaze. "Sorry. Didn't mean to put a damper on things…"

"No worries," Justine said, placing a hand on his arm.

His head jerked at the unexpected touch and his heart did a flip at the genuine caring in her voice. And in her gaze. She looked so sweet and natural, with her hair in that ponytail. Cheeks that looked as soft and rosy as a peach. Eyes that he could swim in.

He found himself drawing closer. She blinked but didn't move away.

He wanted nothing more than to kiss her. And, he could be wrong, but he thought she looked like she wouldn't have a problem with it. But he had a feeling that kissing Justine Winter now would not be wise. He had tasted those lips before, and he knew that once their lips touched it would be sheer torture to break away.

"I have to go," he murmured, looking deep into her eyes.

He wished he didn't, but he had a few things to do before his guests arrived. He saw the warmth in her eyes fading, and she withdrew her hand from his arm. He stood up and Luna, who had fallen asleep, stirred and jumped off the couch. Casson went back into the kitchen to get his hoodie and his keys, and then, nodding to Justine, headed for the door.

"Casson…"

He stopped and turned around. She was steps away, the fingers of both hands tucked into the front pockets of her Capri pants. "Thank you for…for staying the night."

He smiled. "My pleasure."

He opened the door and Luna bounded off.

Justine watched Casson and Luna get into Casson's truck, then returned to the kitchen, her thoughts turning to Robert. She had been such a bleeding heart, letting him in. But he had looked so tormented…and his apology *had* seemed genuine.

It was now obvious that in the time since she had resigned Robert had come apart. She had never known him to drink to excess, but last night he had revealed a different side to him. His alcohol-tinged breath, his unrelenting hold on her… She felt a shudder go through her again at the thought of what might have happened.

His divorce must have been harder for him to deal with than she had realized. Perhaps losing his wife and trying to adjust to all the changes afterward had been too much, inducing him to seek solace in the bottle.

Justine sighed. Robert was a fine lawyer, but even the finest lawyers were not immune to emotional collapse.

She inhaled and exhaled deeply. Could she believe he meant what he had said? He would leave and never come back? Justine had caught so many emotions in that look he'd given her at the door: regret, shame, embarrassment, despair. And fear. Most likely fear that Casson would press charges. Which meant that Robert wasn't so far gone that he no longer cared about his work, his livelihood.

Maybe what had happened last night would be his wake-up call and he'd get help before his life spun completely out of control.

Justine bit on her lower lip. Countless times after she had resigned she'd wished she had explained to Robert how devastated she had felt at his infidelity. Betrayed. *Used.* How she had cried herself to sleep for days. How she'd half hoped he'd come after her and beg for forgiveness. And how, in her darkest moments, she'd thought that when he did she'd forgive him and they would start fresh…

But a month had passed, and then two more after her return to Winter's Haven, and Robert had never once attempted to call, let alone ask for forgiveness.

Seeing him last night had been *her* wake-up call, and she realized that deep down she had never known the true Robert. How could she ever put her trust in him again? No, she had no illusions about starting over with him, or of him being any part of her 'happy-ever-after.' And after the merry-go-round of emotions she had been through she wasn't ready to trust anyone else…

Justine started as she heard a knock on the door. Her stomach gave a lurch, and then she saw that it was Casson. Relieved, she opened the door.

"Luna sent me back," he said, a twinkle in his eye. "She'd like you to join us."

Her eyebrows lifted and she just blinked at him wordlessly.

"I need to drive to Huntsville to pick up a couple of things. Why don't you join me? *Us.* Luna says she's getting bored with my company. And with Spanish guitar music," he added with a deep chuckle. "Besides…you might just discover I'm not the man you think I am."

Justine's pulse had quickened at Casson's very first words. She was tempted to accept his offer, to let a fresh country drive distract her from what had happened with Robert, but… But was it wise to spend time with Casson, given the reason why he was here at Winter's Haven in the first place?

And given her undeniable attraction to him?

Luna barked from the open window and she couldn't help her mouth quirking into a smile.

Although she was well aware that her heart and mind were battling over her decision, she threw caution to the wind. "Tell Luna I'm in," she said, wondering why she sounded so breathless. "I'll just grab my handbag."

Casson had his window partially rolled down. Every once in a while he snuck a glance in Justine's direction. Luna had graciously given up her spot for her and was now in the back seat, head uplifted to enjoy the breeze. Justine alternated between looking out at the scenery and resting back against the leather headrest, her eyes closed and her lips curved in a relaxed smile.

His intuition had been right. She needed to get away from Winter's Haven—even if only for a few hours.

He was all too aware of her proximity: the curve of her peachy cheekbones tapering to her glossy lips, her fitted pink T-shirt rising and falling with her every breath, and her shapely legs so tantalizingly close to his own that every time he manipulated the stick-shift his hand came close to skimming her thigh. He didn't know what was louder: the thrum of the engine or the thrum in his chest.

Casson had to force himself to concentrate on the road several times, and after a stretch on the main highway southbound to Toronto, took Exit Ramp 213 toward Highway 141 to Huntsville. He felt a sense of contentedness with Justine sitting so close to him, even without music or conversation.

This highway had far less traffic, and Casson maneuvered the truck deftly through the winding turns and up and down the hillsides.

"I'll get us some breakfast when we get to my place."

"Your place?" Justine turned her head sharply to stare at him.

"We won't be long," he said casually. "I just have to pick up a couple of things."

He turned on a radio channel of classic rock tunes.

"Are you okay with this?"

At her nod, he cranked it up a bit and, grinning, pressed on the gas pedal.

CHAPTER TEN

JUSTINE'S PULSE POUNDED along with the bass of the stereo. She had enjoyed the quiet, but now welcomed the distraction of music and the kind of songs that she would ordinarily sing to while driving. Her feet and fingers tapped along automatically, and she had to consciously restrain herself from swaying to the music.

She stole a glance at him. The sun beaming down through the windshield and into his truck highlighted the soft golden-brown fuzz on Casson's forearms. His fingers tapped a beat on the steering wheel, and as the muscles in his arms flexed Justine's pulse quickened at the memory of those strong hands and arms carrying her to bed…

Justine was familiar with this route from when she had business in Huntsville, and always loved the views of the myriad sparkling lakes in the Muskokas, but somehow on this trip she barely noticed Lake Rosseau, Horseshoe Lake and Skeleton Lake, among others, and was surprised when Casson turned off the radio to announce that they were coming to Fairy Lake.

Soon Casson was driving through a winding stretch of woodland, with pinpoints of light sparkling through crowns of maple, birch, and pine. Eventually he turned into a long, paved driveway that she thought would never end. But when it finally did Justine couldn't help letting out a gasp. The house—no, *the estate*—was massive, with four dormer windows on the upper level, a wrap-around deck that seemed to equal the circumference of a football field, a four-car garage, and a view that could only be described as heaven, with Fairy Lake a brilliant blue reflecting millions of sun specks.

Justine was still gawking when Casson held the door open for her, and she climbed out, with Luna bounding after her. Two vehicles were sparkling in the sun: the silver-green Mustang convertible she had first seen Casson drive, and a heart-stopping red Ferrari Testarossa.

So Casson Forrester liked his toys. And flaunting his success... But did anyone really need four vehicles? She wondered what luxury model was behind the fourth door…

"Welcome to my place," he said.

Justine's eyes widened as she entered the marble foyer that was connected to a massive living area with gleaming maple hardwood floors and floor-to-ceiling windows. The Muskoka stone fireplace was the focal point, around which several luxurious leather couches were arranged. Hanging on the wall above the polished mantel were two paintings, and as Justine approached she saw that she had guessed correctly: one was a Casson and the other a Carmichael. Both depicted stunning Georgian Bay views. On the mantel itself there was a small baseball cap and a miniature red racing car.

So he was sentimental, too.

"Things from your childhood that you couldn't bear to part with?" she said casually.

She turned to see something flicker across Casson's face.

He stared at her wordlessly for a moment. "Those belonged to Franklin," he said finally, his voice breaking at the end.

He picked up the car and Justine bit her lip as she watched him.

"I came back to get his cap; I always take it with me when I return to Georgian Bay—especially when I go fishing... As for the car..." He picked it up and made the wheels spin. "Frankie loved his toy cars, and this was his favorite. Said he was going to get one when he grew up." His jaw muscles flicked. "Well, I got one for him..."

Justine felt something deflate inside her and her heart felt heavy. He hadn't bought the Ferrari as a status symbol, but as a way of honoring his brother's dream. Guilt washed over her. She wanted to apologize to Casson for being so judgmental, and then she remembered she hadn't voiced her feelings about him flaunting his success.

She gulped. Maybe she shouldn't let her feelings about Robert cloud her judgment about Casson. Maybe she should stop lumping them into the same box...

"Okay..." Casson pressed his lips together. "Let's lighten things up. How about I make you a light and fluffy omelet?"

His mouth curved into a smile and he motioned

for her to continue into the kitchen at the other end of the room.

Justine nodded, and was instantly wowed by the chef's kitchen with its stunning curved granite island the color of sapphire, plush stools, and at least double the amount of cupboards she had, with a sturdy harvest table in the dining area that she was sure could comfortably sit twenty.

She sat on a stool and watched Casson in T-shirt and jeans, the muscles in his arms flexing with his every movement. Her heartbeat did an erratic dance…

Had he just said something to her? She stared at him blankly.

His mouth quirked, an eyebrow lifted, and he waved the spatula in his hand. "Wanna get the toast?"

"Sure."

Avoiding his gaze, she slid off the stool and put the toast on. *He must lift weights*, she thought, edging a glance at his arms as he flipped the omelets. *Or else he regularly lifts two-by-fours at his hardware stores.*

The sudden image of him wearing nothing but

jeans and steel-toed boots, pumping a stack of wood, made her insides blaze.

Casson slid the omelets onto two plates, and Justine buttered the toast. He poured coffee into two mugs and sat down next to her.

"Bon appétit," he said, his eyes crinkling at her as he tasted the omelet. "Not bad."

"Delicious," she agreed.

"I'll believe it after you've had a bite." He looked pointedly at her untouched portion.

Justine could have kicked herself. *Good one.*

"I mean it *looks* delicious," she said lightly, gazing down at her plate.

His leg was almost touching hers, and she tried not to think about it, or about the way his jeans fit, and the way his arms looked, so smooth and bronzed.

Like a sculpture that you just wanted to stroke...

"More coffee?" His voice melded with her thoughts.

She turned her head, her stomach tightening at how close his face was to hers. His eyes were like shiny chestnuts, with flecks of gold around his dark pupils.

"Yes...please..." she managed, and then concentrated on eating her omelet.

* * *

Casson waited until Justine was finished and then offered to take her on a tour of the rest of the house. He started with his study on the main floor, and he could see that she loved it, unconsciously stroking the gleaming surface of his mahogany desk and pausing to peruse the volumes in his floor-to-ceiling bookshelves.

She turned to fix him with a crooked smile. “Is this a lending library?” she said, a teasing glint in her eye.

“Only for—”

“Oh!”

She had caught sight of the mahogany spiral staircase in one corner.

“That leads up to my bedroom,” he said, as casually as he could. “When I can’t sleep I like to spend time down here with my literary friends.” He gestured toward the bookshelves.

Casson had a sudden vision of Justine in a silk robe, reading a book in his Italian leather recliner and then gliding up the staircase…

He gave himself a mental shake and suggested they go to the upper level. He ordered Luna to stay, and then walked out of the room and up another flight of stairs. He led Justine through two luxurious guest bedrooms, and then the guest bathroom, repressing his desire to smile as her eyes popped at the sight of the transparent walls of his shower stall, with its back wall designed to be the center part of a larger window overlooking the lake and hills. The enormous claw-foot bathtub looked out at the same view.

He proceeded toward the huge double doors leading to his bedroom. "Don't worry," he said in a conspiratorial tone, "I don't have any nefarious intentions. It's just that this room has one of the best views of the lake."

If Justine had been impressed by his study and bathroom, he could tell she was blown away by his bedroom, with its rustic four-poster king-sized bed, cottage-style dressers, pine-green and forest-themed linens, the huge walk-in closet, massive custom-built windows and a set of sliding doors. They opened on to a semi-circular deck that spanned from one end of the house to the other, with a hot tub in one corner and a screened-in sunroom with lounging chairs and a bar. And a pull-out couch.

"For those summer nights when I'd rather sleep outside," he murmured.

"Oh…my…" Justine looked out at the sparkling waters of Fairy Lake. "I… I have never seen anything like this. You must hate to leave this place," she said, glancing back at him.

He gave her a measured look. "It serves its purpose…" He hesitated, and wondered if he should tell Justine that, much as he loved his home, he felt that something was missing. Or maybe a special *someone.* But, no, there was no reason for him to go there.

He had learned to keep his thoughts and feelings in check since his childhood. Maybe he even shied away from serious relationships, from love, because of the trauma of losing his brother, and in some ways his parents as well.

Why would he do anything differently now and suddenly open up to Justine? Reveal all his thoughts, hopes and dreams to her? Share the real reason for his resort venture? Although he may have cracked a bit, telling her about Franklin's cap and toy car, he had no intention of ending up like Humpty Dumpty.

She walked to the edge of the deck and, looking over, gasped again.

He caught up to her and followed her gaze to the ground level, beyond the salmon-colored interlocking patio to a huge kidney-shaped swimming pool. Around it the lush landscaped lawns and gardens featured flowering bushes, working fountains and lounging areas. A white gazebo stood close to the waterfront, along with a half-dozen Muskoka chairs around a fire-pit.

A man trimming the hedges by the gazebo looked up at them and waved before leaving the grounds.

"That's Phillip, my gardener, groundskeeper, car maintenance man and all-around good guy," he said, waving back. "I lucked out when I found him. And his wife Sue. She does the housekeeping and provides me with an occasional dinner when I don't want to batch it," he said, grinning at Justine.

"With a place like this, I'm surprised you have to *batch it* at all..."

The words were out before Justine could stop them. She felt her face igniting at her implication that women would seek his company only for his material possessions.

"I'm sorry. I didn't mean to imply—"

"That the ladies are all over me just for my hot tub and my pool?" He laughed. "I generally don't have time to do a lot of *that kind* of entertaining. My business ventures keep my hands tied. Although..." he raised his eyebrows and his tawny eyes pierced hers "...I occasionally *un*tie my hands..."

Justine's heart began to palpitate and she looked away. How could she even begin to respond? And what was this sharp twist in her stomach at the thought of his hands on another woman? In the hot tub and sharing his bed?

She felt pinned under Casson's gaze. Sensed he had moved closer. She couldn't help but breathe in his fresh pine scent, and when she tentatively looked back at him his lips were suddenly on hers, his arms bracing her against him. She gasped, and felt all her muscles slacken. Closing her eyes, she surrendered to the desire pumping through her. Pressing her hand against the back of his head, she responded hungrily as he deepened his kiss.

And then she felt him break away from her, so suddenly that she almost lost her balance.

"I'm sorry," he said gruffly. "I didn't intend to—"

"Neither did I," she said in a rush. "We should go in…"

When they were back on the main floor, Casson strode over to the fireplace and took Franklin's cap.

"This is what I came for," he said lightly. "And the Mustang. I won't be needing my truck for a while."

Justine was glad Casson had slipped in a Spanish guitar CD. Luna didn't seem to mind it at all, and had fallen asleep in the back seat. Justine closed her eyes, wishing she could fall asleep herself. It was so awkward now…especially in the more intimate confines of his Mustang.

She looked out her window, forcing herself not to steal glances at Casson. When he swerved slightly to avoid a porcupine she found herself pinned against him for a moment, and her heart flipped at the proximity of his firm lips…

Her thoughts tumbled about during the rest of the drive. And when Casson switched the music to Pachelbel's *Canon in D*, Justine felt herself swept up by the sensual strains of the violins and *basso continuo*, closing her eyes as the wind ruffled her hair.

As the Mustang started to slow down before turning in to Winter's Haven, Justine realized she must have dozed off. She asked Casson to drop her off by the office, and when he did, scrambled out of the car before he could get the door for her. He shrugged and got back into his seat.

"Thanks for the drive and breakfast." She managed a weak smile.

Two teenagers from one of the cottages rode by on their bikes and waved.

"Hey, mister," one called out, coming to a stop not far from the Mustang, its silver-green exterior and chrome sparkling in the sun. "She's a beauty!"

Casson removed his sunglasses and met Justine's gaze. "She sure is," he said softly. And then he turned and gave a thumbs-up to the boy.

Something swirled inside of Justine and spiraled up to her chest.

Had he just paid her a compliment? Or was the sunlight addling her brain?

Casson's car thrummed as he started the ignition, made a sleek turn and drove away. When he was out of sight Justine walked back to her place, needing the time to replay the events of the morning with Casson. She caught sight of the coffee mugs, and as she filled the sink with soapy water Justine felt herself burning with curiosity about his guests.

Well, she'd find out soon enough.

She dried her hands and walked over to look at *Mirror Lake*. She had always loved it, with its undulating hills, their stunning colors reflected in the glassy surface of the lake. Hues of green, purple, gold, red and blue, blending in sensuous curves and prismatic streaks across the hilly landscape. A feast for the eyes.

Looking at it now, she felt a lump in her throat, thinking of Casson's brother Franklin suffering at such a young age, and of his family, suffering along with him, all in their different ways. *Poor Casson.* He had been nine when Franklin was diagnosed and ten when Franklin died. *Ten!* Her heart ached when she thought of how Franklin's passing must have changed their lives. And how Casson was still honoring his brother's memory all these years later.

She had witnessed a hint of Casson's vulnerability when he'd told her about Franklin's cap and toy car, and she felt renewed remorse at her earlier thought that he had bought the Ferrari as a status symbol. Maybe Casson had been right… *He wasn't the man she'd thought he was.*

Justine had sensed that Casson was unwilling to open up any further and share more details of his past to her. *And why should he?* She didn't trust his motives when it came to Winter's Haven—and Casson was well aware of this—so why should *he* trust *her?*

She tore her gaze away from the painting and went upstairs.

By the time she'd got out of the shower and let her hair dry naturally outside on the deck, it was almost noon. She biked over to the office and while she waited for Mandy to finish a call, quickly checked the register and saw the names "Ronnie and Andy Walsh" listed as Casson's guests.

Mandy got off the phone, and Justine briefly told her what had happened with Robert.

Mandy's mouth dropped. "Thank goodness Casson came to your rescue," she said, her eyes wide. "And Luna! Talk about great timing!" She gave Justine a tight hug. "I'm so glad you're okay."

Mandy shot a glance toward the diner entrance.

"Your hero is in there," she said in a conspiratorial tone. "Having lunch with his guests. Oh, here they come!"

Justine looked casually over her shoulder. Casson was laughing, with a guest on either side of him. Not two brothers, as she had expected. A good-looking woman and a boy of no more than five or six. *'Ronnie' was a woman.* And the boy—it had to be her son—must be Andy.

The three of them looked like a family. As they approached, Justine tried to ignore the sinking sensation in the pit of her stomach, and she hoped her smile didn't appear as fake as it felt.

CHAPTER ELEVEN

CASSON HAD HIS arm around Ronnie's shoulder and was holding Andy's hand. Ronnie was a petite brunette, with a perky haircut that emphasized the fine bone structure of her face. She wore faded jeans and a retro-style cotton top with short gathered sleeves and a splashy flower print. Her running shoes were lime-green.

Tiny but not afraid to roar, Justine couldn't help thinking, unable to prevent a blistering sensation from coursing through her. *Was it jealousy?* She wished she could hide, but it was too late.

The little boy—Andy—was small, too. He wore a Toronto Blue Jays cap and a red and white T-shirt and jean shorts, and his skinny little legs moved quickly to keep up with the adults. He kept smiling up at Casson, and occasionally tugged at his hand.

Justine couldn't make out their conversation, but as they approached heard Andy saying something about catching a big fish. Casson threw back his head and let out a deep laugh, and Justine felt her stomach twist at the intimate scene the trio presented.

Mandy went back to her desk to accept a delivery, and Justine stood there awkwardly, knowing how strange it would look if she suddenly left.

She wished she had never decided to come to the diner for lunch. Somehow, her appetite was gone.

Casson was still smiling when they reached Justine, but his arm was no longer encircling Ronnie's waist. "Let me introduce my guests," he said. "Justine Winter, this is Veronica Walsh and her little fisherman Andy." He grinned down at the boy. "He says he wants to catch a *big* one while he's here."

Although he was pale, with dark shadows under his green eyes, Andy's elfin grin made his freckled face light up.

"Nice to meet you, Andy." She held out her hand and was pleased when he shook it and nodded.

"Nice to meet you too, Miss Winter," he said, looking up directly at her.

Justine smiled, impressed at his communication skills. She turned to Veronica. "I hope you enjoy Winter's Haven, Veronica."

What else could she say?

Veronica held out her hand, and for a tiny person her handshake was surprisingly strong.

"Please call me Ronnie." She smiled, her eyes crinkling warmly. "Everyone does—except for Casson, when he wants to be formal. Or when he's scolding me." She laughed. "You have a lovely place, Justine," she said, waving her arm in an arc. "Casson was right. He told me it was enchanting."

Justine avoided looking at Casson.

Of course he finds it enchanting; that's why he wants to take it off my hands.

Justine hoped her cynicism didn't show through in her smile, which was starting to waver.

"Hey, Cass," Andy pulled at Casson's hand. "When can we go fishing?"

Cass? It was obvious this was no ordinary relationship for Andy to be using this nickname. Justine watched as Casson's eyes lit up again as he looked down on the boy.

"You've just barely arrived and you're hounding me already!" He chuckled. "Speaking of hounds—there's one waiting for you in Cottage Number One."

"Luna!" Andy tugged at Casson's hand. "Let's go, Cass. I can't wait to play tag with her! We can go fishing after that!"

"Bossy little thing, eh?" Casson's smile took in Ronnie and Justine. "I have a feeling I won't have a moment's peace while this munchkin is here. Hey, there, Andrew Michael Walsh." He feigned a stern glance at Andy. "If you pull my hand any harder it'll fall off—and I won't be able to fish with one hand."

Andy giggled. "Then we'll have to take *her* with us, since Mommy doesn't like to fish."

Justine flushed, not knowing what to say.

Ronnie burst out laughing. "Andy's right. All I want to catch while I'm here are some rays." She looked up at Casson and winked. "We'll settle into the cottage while you go and get Luna's food at the vet's." She turned to Justine. "Nice meeting you!"

As Ronnie's car turned the bend and disappeared Justine's mind launched a battle inside her brain's hemispheres of reason and judgment.

Casson obviously had no scruples—kissing *her* during the storm, and again at his house, when all along he had a significant other.

How uncouth of him! Despicable, really, when the relationship involved a child.

A child who obviously adored him.

The more she thought about it, the more her stomach twisted at the thought of Casson deceiving Ronnie and continuing to allow Andy to become attached to him. If he and Ronnie broke up Andy would undoubtedly be heartbroken. Casson's underhandedness, his toying with the emotions of both Ronnie and Andy, was reprehensible.

He was toying with you, too...

She cringed.

And you enjoyed his charms...

"Are you all right?" Casson had turned to face her. "You looked like you were in pain..."

Justine caught a whiff of his cologne, its now familiar woodsy scent. She so wanted to give him a blast for being a cad, but the concern in his voice made her hesitate. And then she recalled the look of trust in Andy's eyes, the hero-worship...

"I'm fine," she heard herself reply coldly as his hand cupped her under one elbow.

She stepped away from him, trying not to make it obvious that she didn't welcome his touch. She swayed slightly and he reached out again. The pressure of both his hands on her bare arms sent a shiver rippling through her.

"Maybe the heat is getting to you," he murmured. "I'll grab you a bottle of water from the diner—"

"I can get it myself," she said curtly, and then, more politely, "Thanks."

Casson let go of her, gazed at her for what seemed longer than necessary, and then strode to his car. Afraid that he would turn around and see the conflicting emotions on her face, she fled into the office.

Mandy was preoccupied with a jam in the printer, and Justine was glad she had a few moments to compose herself.

She glanced out the window and watched Casson drive off, an ache blooming in her chest. Ronnie and Andy were only here for the weekend, but it sounded like they were going to have a great time with Casson.

"I'm not surprised he's taken," Mandy murmured. "But they're not engaged; I didn't notice any ring on her finger." She came around from the printer to look at Justine thoughtfully. "Hey, girl, this is your day off. Get thee to a beach. I hear there's a great one right here at Winter's Haven. And after all you've been through you need some serious relaxation."

Justine avoided looking directly at Mandy. The last thing she wanted was to show how emotional she felt, especially with some of the other cottagers now coming out of the diner.

"Yeah, I think I'll do just that," she said lightly.

Leaving the office, Justine got on her bike and pedaled furiously back to her place. Sweating, she peeled off her clothes in the upstairs washroom and got into a one-piece coral swimsuit. After slapping on some sunscreen, she grabbed a beach bag and threw in a book, an oversized beach towel, a small cushion and a bottle of water. With sunglasses and a floppy beach hat, she headed to the beach.

With any luck the cool waters of the bay would extinguish the blaze consuming her, body and soul.

* * *

On his drive to and from the town, Casson couldn't stop thinking about Justine's aloofness. And the way she had recoiled from his touch. If he had imagined it the first time he had extended his hand to her elbow, her reaction the second time around had left no doubt in his mind about her feelings. Yet she hadn't resisted his touch during the storm and after he'd kicked Robert out of her house last night…or this morning at his place…

Something twisted in his gut. Maybe Justine was only just beginning to process the traumatic impact of Robert's intrusion and attempted sexual assault. And was transferring her feelings of fear and distrust to *him*.

He had felt his own stomach muscles tighten when he'd gone to return Robert's car to him earlier. Robert had come to the door, his face pale and his eyes puffy, with dark shadows. After ascertaining that he was sober, Casson had handed him his car keys with a terse reminder of the promise he had made to Justine. Robert had apologized for the trouble he had caused, and with a look of resignation driven away.

Casson frowned. Justine hadn't trusted him to begin with. How on earth could he make that change now?

He strode into the cottage and plunked Luna's bag of dog kibble in a corner of the entrance. He couldn't help grinning at the sight of Andy and Luna in the living room, Andy giggling every time Luna licked his cheek. He ducked and feigned trying to escape, Luna skittering around him.

While Ronnie got Andy settled upstairs in the loft Casson prepared a couple of wine spritzers and brought them into the living room. His thoughts turned to Justine again. The feel of her in his arms… The look of her in her nightie…and in the turquoise swimsuit he had first seen her in.

He felt a swirl of heat radiate throughout his body and took a long gulp of his spritzer. He wanted her property, yes—but, like it or not, his body was telling him that he wanted *her*, too. There was absolutely no chance of *that* happening, though. He couldn't imagine that Justine would allow herself to trust him enough to share his bed.

Despite his attraction to Justine—no, he had

to be honest with himself and call it what it was: his almost constant torturous desire that was aching for release—he had business to take care of. Contractors waiting. Timelines and deadlines. He had to find the opportune moment to bring up the property issue, and to convince Justine to sell.

If things went his way, he anticipated sealing the deal by the end of his "holiday" at Winter's Haven. But for now his plan would have to wait, until after Ronnie and Andy left.

While he waited for Ronnie to join him he tried to justify to himself why he couldn't tell Justine the real reason he wanted the Russell properties and Winter's Haven.

Maybe because that would make him vulnerable... And maybe he wasn't quite ready to reveal that side of himself to her...yet.

CHAPTER TWELVE

JUSTINE COULDN'T STOP thinking about Casson's guests. They were obviously very good friends, judging from his use of their nicknames. Veronica—Justine couldn't bring herself to call her Ronnie—was very pretty, confident, and seemed the type to say what she wanted to say. And from what she could see Andy was a polite little boy who had been taught good social skills.

It was obvious he loved "Cass." And for him to have developed a relationship with Casson they must have spent a lot of time together. Which meant Casson had spent even *more* time with his mother.

Justine felt something jab at her insides. She stopped and brushed the remnants of beach sand from her legs. *What did she expect?* That a gorgeous, successful entrepreneur like Casson Forrester would be unattached? *And why should she care?*

His intentions were not on par with hers when it came to Winter's Haven. She shouldn't even be trusting him, given his manipulative way of getting himself onto her property. And after Robert's infidelity she'd vowed she wouldn't offer her trust to any other man so easily in the future.

But you trusted Casson to stay over in case Robert came back...

Yes, she had. And he had comforted her too. Made her breakfast at his place. *Kissed her.* And while he had been doing all those things Justine had forgotten what Casson was really here for.

Justine reached the house and went up to shower. She had spent more time than she'd originally planned on the beach. After a refreshing swim in the bay she had dried off on the chaise lounge and drifted to sleep, listening to the waves lap against the shore.

Now she towel-dried her hair and slipped into a pair of white denim shorts and a flowered halter top. She went down to the kitchen and grabbed a lemon-lime soda, and decided to make herself a tuna and tomato sandwich on walnut bread.

She checked the clock. She had a feeling it was going to be a long evening and night.

After finishing her sandwich, she went out to water her vegetable and flower gardens with the hose that was connected to a pump in the bay. Ordinarily she loved doing this—it was part of her morning and evening routine—but tonight she did it perfunctorily, lost in her thoughts.

A sudden bark startled her and she turned. Casson jumped back and Luna skittered away, barking at the offending spray of water. Justine dropped the hose and stared at Casson helplessly as he pinched his drenched shirt and pulled it away from his chest.

"I'm *so* sorry," she told him.

Luna came bounding toward her, now that she had relinquished her water weapon, and Justine patted her and glanced edgewise at Casson.

"I can get you a towel..." she offered contritely.

"If you insist," he drawled. "The funny thing is, I was coming to see you about getting a couple of extra towels for Ronnie and Andy. I was supposed to go back to the office earlier for some, but Ronnie and I got to talking, and then once Andy had a rest we spent the rest of the afternoon on the beach. It wasn't until after supper that I realized I had forgotten. By that time the office was closed."

His eyes narrowed as he spoke, and Justine could feel his gaze lowering over her body.

"I see that you were out on the beach as well," he said, starting to undo the top buttons of his shirt.

Justine frowned. *How would he know that?*

"You're more tanned than the last time I saw you," he said dryly.

He finished undoing all his buttons and flapped the wet panels of his shirt away from his body. Justine's gaze slid down and she caught a glimpse of his chest and sculpted abs. She felt her pulse accelerating, sparking an invigorating trail along her nerve-endings. When her glance moved upward she was mortified to find that Casson was well aware of her visual exploration.

"Yes, it was a perfect day to relax on the beach," she said, a little too brightly. "I hope your guests enjoyed it also?"

"Oh, they did. Andy and Luna had fun kicking a ball around before splashing about in the bay, and Ronnie enjoyed lying in the sun before her swim."

Justine wished he hadn't gone into detail. She didn't *want* to picture Veronica lying there in a bikini while Casson spread sunscreen all over her. But her mind had a will of its own, and she began to think of what he and Veronica might have been doing while Andy and Luna were playing…

Kissing, maybe. She'd have run her hands over the soft fuzz on his chest…

"I'd appreciate you lending us some extra towels."

His voice nudged her back to the present, and she nodded. "I'll only be a minute. You can wait in the porch if you'd like."

"Oh, by the way," Casson added as she opened the inner door. "I had another reason for coming by…"

Justine turned, and there was something in his voice that made her wonder if it had to do with Robert's departure. Or selling Winter's Haven.

She looked at him suspiciously, her guard up.

"If you haven't made other plans, you're welcome to join us for a campfire. I picked up a bag of marshmallows for Andy." He grinned and his gaze swept over her. "But you might want to change into something more substantial," he said, his gaze lingering on her exposed shoulders. "I don't want the mosquitoes to attack you when it gets dark."

Justine first thought was to decline. She couldn't imagine being the fourth wheel around the campfire.

What would they talk about? And did Veronica know that he was inviting her?

And then she heard her own traitorous voice murmuring casually, "Sure, why not?" before she flew in to get some towels, her heart a jackhammer.

Justine's acceptance took Casson by complete surprise. He'd been sure Justine was going to turn down his invitation. Earlier, she had been courteous enough to Ronnie and Andy, but Casson had detected a slight resistance on her part to over-extend herself.

He'd thought about it on the beach this afternoon while Ronnie had sunbathed and Andy had played with Luna. He'd tried to put himself in her shoes, having to put up with someone who had manipulated—though he would say *master-minded*—his way into Winter's Haven.

Of course Justine would be on the defensive—not only with *him*, but maybe even with his guests. Or rather *guest*. He wasn't an expert on female psychology, but he had sensed a bit of tension from Justine. Maybe it was the way she had glanced edgewise at Ronnie and stood there a little awkwardly, her cheeks like pink blossoms.

Luna flopped down on Justine's entrance mat. "Make yourself at home." Casson chuckled. "Although I might as well do the same."

He made himself comfortable on a padded wicker chair—or as comfortable as he could be with a wet shirt that kept sticking to him—and a minute later Justine reemerged. She had changed into a red T-shirt and a navy hoodie and sweat pants. Her lipstick was the same shade as her top—a cherry-red that activated his pulse. She handed him a towel and placed a big nautical-style beach bag on the wicker chair next to him before bending down to put on her running shoes.

Luna ambled over to lick her face, making Justine lose her balance. Casson dropped his towel and leaped forward to help her straighten up. He heard her quick intake of breath and wanted nothing more than to lean forward and seal those lips with his own.

Taste their fruity nectar.

Unable to stop himself, he began to move his face toward hers…

Justine pulled away as if she had been jolted by an electric current. Something shifted in his expression and he gave her a curt smile.

"We'd better be going. Andy gets tired quickly, and usually has an early bedtime, but he won't leave me in peace until I make him a campfire and we have a marshmallow roast."

Justine nodded and saw his gaze drop to her beach bag. "A flashlight for when I walk back home," she said. "And the extra towels you asked for."

As they started walking Justine diverted her thoughts to what Casson had said about Andy getting tired and having a rest earlier. Most little boys his age had boundless energy. Many of the cottagers at Winter's Haven had kids staying, and they tore around like little hellions—often to the consternation of their parents.

"I noticed that Andy seems a little…fragile," she said, trying to break the awkward silence. "He must have had a late night before the drive here this morning; he has such dark shadows under his eyes."

Casson didn't respond. Justine bit her lip, wondering if she had sounded judgmental.

They continued to walk in silence along the road, Luna beside Casson. Justine kept her eyes on the sun-dappled shadows of the pines.

Suddenly Casson slowed his steps and turned to look at her. "It wasn't because he had a late night," he said, an edge creeping into his voice. "It's because he has cancer."

Justine felt waves of shock rippling through her body. For a few moments she couldn't move. Or speak. She stared up at Casson and knew her face must reveal the questions she wanted to ask but couldn't bring herself to for fear of sounding insensitive.

"He's in remission and undergoing maintenance chemo," Casson said. "His treatment has taken a lot out of him—*and* Ronnie—but he's a tough little guy, despite the impression he may give with those skinny little legs and body. He's got a lot of spirit…"

His voice wavered and Justine felt her heart breaking.

Casson looked away and continued walking. "He had some dizzy spells and nosebleeds when he was four," he said as Justine caught up to him. "And he was getting headaches. When he had a seizure with a high fever they did some tests and he was brought immediately to Toronto's Hospital for Sick Children, where they started chemotherapy—which took months. Once Andy was in remission they started maintenance chemo. He's now in his second year of that."

"Poor child…" Jasmine squeezed her eyes so she wouldn't cry, but felt a teardrop trickle down anyway. "And his poor parents." She shook her head. "I can't even imagine what they must have been going through…"

Casson didn't offer any further details, and Justine didn't feel it was appropriate to ply him with questions, so they walked in silence again.

No wonder Andy looked so gaunt beneath his baseball cap.

She didn't remember seeing any hair around his

temples, but had just assumed that he had gotten a summer buzz cut.

Justine felt sorry for Veronica. How heart-wrenching it must have been for her to hear that her only child was afflicted with a disease that could take his life.

And what about Andy's father? Where was he? And what exactly was the relationship between Veronica and Casson?

It must have been devastating for Casson to learn of Andy's diagnosis as well—especially after having lost his brother to leukemia.

These thoughts and more kept swirling in her mind. She had been able to tell from that first meeting this morning that Casson had a special relationship with Andy. And with Andy's mother. They looked like a happy family, vacationing together and doing all the things that families did.

So why was *she* being invited to take part in their evening? If Casson and Veronica were more than just friends, wouldn't he want to spend the evening alone with her? Okay, Andy was with them, but he'd eventually go to bed…

Justine had no intention of asking Casson to enlighten her about any of these questions. They had arrived at the cottage and Andy was opening the screen door in excitement, holding the bag of marshmallows.

Casson's face lit up immediately. Seeing him like that made Justine choke up. She hoped she could keep it together now that she knew about Andy's condition. She smiled at Andy and he smiled back and waved before attempting to open up the bag.

"Hey, hold on a minute, kid!" Casson chuckled. "Let me get the fire going. If you open the bag now there won't be any left to roast."

"Aw, Cass, I promise I'll just have one..." Andy grinned.

"And I'll be watching him like a hawk to make sure," his mother said, emerging from the cottage. She greeted Justine with a smile. "So nice you could join us, Justine."

"Hi, Veronica." Justine returned the smile, not wanting to reveal how uncomfortable she was.

"Please." Veronica grinned at her as she came down the cottage steps. "It's Ronnie, remember? Only my mother calls me by my full name."

Justine laughed. "Okay—Ronnie. By the way,

here are the towels." She pulled them out of her beach bag.

"Great—thank you." Ronnie took them and before opening the door said, "Can I get you a drink before we head down to the beach? I'm having white wine, but I can mix you a margarita, if you like, or a martini. I make a wicked chocolate martini!"

"Oh…um…a little white wine would be fine…"

"Great. How about you, Cass? A margarita?" she said teasingly.

Casson made a face. "I'll have a nice cold beer, thank you. A good Canadian lager for a good Canadian boy."

Ronnie let out a belly laugh. "*Andy's* a good Canadian boy. *You*—I'm not so sure." She turned to her son. "What can I get you, sweetie? How about some lemonade?"

"Sure, Mom," Andy replied distractedly, busy helping Casson gather twigs from the bushes nearby and putting them in a large canvas bag.

"Hey, Ronnie!" Casson grinned. "Would you mind grabbing me a T-shirt and my hoodie? I don't want to get eaten alive by mosquitoes down by the water."

"Is there anything *I* can do?" Justine said after Ronnie had gone to get the drinks.

Casson turned and looked at her. *For a little too long.*

"You can help Ronnie bring down the drinks," he said finally, a gleam in his eyes. "Andy and I will head down to the beach and get the fire started. Ready, partner?" he asked the boy.

"Ready!" Andy nodded excitedly.

His baseball cap fell off, and Justine felt a twinge in her heart at the sight of Andy's shaved head. She watched them walking away, Casson's muscular frame next to Andy's little body, Luna bounding ahead of them. She could see that Casson was deliberately walking slowly so Andy could keep up with him.

He's a good guy, an inner voice whispered.

Justine shivered, even though the night air was balmy. She remembered how upset she had been after their first meeting in the office, and how rattled when he'd let himself into her house with Luna. And when she'd stumbled and fallen into his lap…

But she couldn't deny that he had some good qualities. He had stayed the night in case Robert came back, hadn't he? And the way he interacted with Andy, you'd swear he was the boy's father. *That's how a father should be,* she mused.

Another thought occurred to her. Could it be that Ronnie was divorced and Casson was potentially her next husband?

"Hey, Justine, can you give me a hand with this wine and the glasses? I'll bring the beer and the pitcher of lemonade. And Casson's clothes."

"Sure."

Justine stepped up to the door. She took the tray and held the door open for Ronnie.

As they walked down the path to the beach Ronnie said softly, "Isn't Casson something? He goes above and beyond when it comes to Andy… He's told you about Andy's condition?" She glanced at Justine.

"Yes." Justine felt Ronnie's gaze and turned to meet it. "I was so sorry to hear about that," she said simply. "I can't imagine what you and Andy have been through."

Ronnie's pace slowed. "I couldn't have done it without Cass. He's not only a great cousin, but an even greater godfather to Andy." Her voice quivered. "We're so blessed to have him in our lives."

Justine's heart was racing. *Cousin? Godfather?*

"He's like a brother—the brother I never had." Ronnie's eyes welled up. "Here I go, getting all weepy again." She blinked the tears away. "Casson's going to be a great dad someday. And an awesome husband for one lucky lady..."

Casson had the fire started by the time Ronnie and Justine got down to the beach. The dry kindling was crackling over crumpled up newspaper. He looked up briefly and nodded at them before arranging thicker branches in a spoke-like configuration. Andy threw in some small twigs occasionally, watching in fascination as the fire crackled and sent out sparks.

There were four Muskoka chairs arranged in a semicircle behind the fire-pit, and in the middle a huge tree stump served as a tabletop. Justine set down the wine and glasses, and Ronnie followed suit with the beer and lemonade.

Casson took off his damp shirt and tossed it onto one of the chairs, before reaching for the T-shirt and hoodie that Ronnie had hooked over her arm and was now holding out to him. Justine was just steps away, and he could tell that she was trying not to glance at his bare torso.

Feeling a rush suffuse his body, he turned away to check the fire.

When the fire was robust, Casson stacked half-logs over the branches and in no time at all the fire was roaring. Feeling the sweat trickling down his face, Casson thanked Ronnie for the beer, and helped himself to a long swig. Ronnie poured Andy a glass of lemonade before filling the wine glasses.

"Here's to summer fun." Ronnie lifted her glass. "Cheers, guys."

Casson tipped his beer bottle to clink with Ronnie's glass. They laughed when Andy clinked his glass with them. When Casson turned to do the same with Justine their gazes locked. Something swirled in the pit of his stomach. Justine's face was mesmerizing in the light and shadows cast by the fire. Her eyes looked like blue ice, and standing so close to her beside the spiraling flames he felt desire flicking through his body.

He wanted her.

With a yearning that stunned him.

Out of the corner of his eye he saw Ronnie and Andy putting marshmallows on the branches

Casson had collected and sharpened earlier. He was glad their attention was diverted, and even more glad that Justine's eyes seemed to be reflecting something he hadn't seen before. In her or in any other woman he had dated.

Maybe it was the romance of a campfire on a starry night, with the dark, silky waters of Georgian Bay just steps away, the soft gushing of their ebb and flow joining with the crackling of the fire. Maybe it was just the fact that Justine was one helluva beautiful woman, and that having already kissed those lips once, he felt the urge to kiss them again.

And again.

It was a good thing, perhaps, that Ronnie and Andy were there, or right now he'd be—

"Hey, Cass!" Andy called. "Come and roast some marshmallows. You too, Justine. Mom went to get me my hoodie."

Casson watched the expression in Justine's eyes change instantly. She gave Andy a bright smile and strode over to pick up a stick and a marshmallow. She laughed at the sight of Andy's sticky face.

A warm feeling came over Casson at the picture they made. Justine seemed so comfortable around Andy. *Natural.* Not stiff, like some of his past dates when he'd introduced them to his godson. Justine was chatting with Andy as if she had always known him. And he was responding in a spirited fashion, bursting into giggles at one point.

She would make a great mother.

A sudden mental image of Justine pregnant, her hands resting gently over her belly, followed almost immediately by a picture of him feeling the mound as well, startled him.

Where were these thoughts coming from?

Casson felt his heartbeat quicken and the sweat start to slide down his temples. He wiped his face with his sleeve and had another gulp of beer before rising.

As the four of them twirled their sticks over the flames Casson stole a glance at Justine. She was the first to be done. She stepped back and, after waving her stick to cool off her perfectly roasted marshmallow, bit into its golden-brown exterior and got to the warm, gooey white center.

"Mmm…heaven…" she said between bites.

She'd got some of the caramel center stuck

around her mouth, and Casson found himself wishing he could lick the stickiness off…

"Hey, Cass, you need to concentrate a little better than that!"

Ronnie's laughing voice reached his ears and, looking away from Justine, he groaned when he realized that his marshmallow had blackened. Shrugging, he set down his stick.

"Here, let me show you how it's done." Justine grinned.

She prepared a new stick and twirled it slowly, until the marshmallow reached a toffee-like color, and then handed it to him. He bit into it, savoring its caramel sweetness, his eyes never leaving her face.

"That," he said, after finishing it off, "was the best marshmallow I've ever had. What do you say, Andy? Should we give Justine the prize for Best Marshmallow?"

Andy nodded vigorously. "But what do we *give* her, Cass?" He cocked his head in puzzlement.

Casson stroked his chin, pretending to look thoughtful. "How about we take her fishing tomorrow?"

"Yeah! Can you come, Justine?" Andy's face lit up. "You won the prize!"

Justine gazed from Andy to Casson and then to Ronnie, who was nodding approvingly.

"Yes—go! I don't fish." Ronnie chuckled. "I just eat."

Casson met Justine's gaze. "You can take us to the hot spots…"

He watched Justine's eyes flicker and her mouth twitch ever so slightly. Her gaze shifted to Andy, who had his little hands in a prayer position and was looking up at her beseechingly.

Her face broke into a big grin. "I guess I can't turn down first prize," she said, reaching down to give Andy a hug.

After they'd feasted on another round of marshmallows Casson walked to the water's edge and filled a couple of large pails. While he extinguished the fire Ronnie and Justine finished what was left of their wine and started gathering up the glasses, bottles and the pitcher of lemonade. They returned to the cottage, and Andy said goodnight to Justine before going inside.

"Well, I'll say goodnight too," Justine said brightly, slinging her beach bag over her arm.

"Thank you for a nice evening. It's been a long time since I roasted marshmallows."

"Goodnight, Justine," Ronnie said, waving. "Andy had fun with you."

"I won't say goodnight just yet," Casson said to Justine when they were alone. "I'm walking you home after I read Andy a story. *And it'll be a short one*," he added huskily.

CHAPTER THIRTEEN

CASSON HAD INVITED her to wait inside the cottage, but Justine had said she'd be fine outside. The night air was warm and the half-moon provided some illumination. She sat on a lawn chair by the front door of the cottage with Luna at her feet. The screen on the door was partially up, and she could faintly hear Casson's voice.

Barely a few minutes had passed when Casson reemerged. "The little guy was wiped," he said. "Couldn't keep his eyes open. By the third page he was out." Casson shrugged. "Come on, Luna." He ruffled her fur briskly. "Time to take Miss *Wintry* home." He flashed Justine a grin.

Justine rose and put up her hand in protest. "I'm a big girl and I can take myself home. Really." She looked at him pointedly. "I won't get lost; it *is* my property." She made herself smile in case she had sounded abrupt. "But, thank you; I appreciate your offer."

Casson's eyes glinted. "I'm not offering. You may know your way around, but I won't be able to sleep wondering if a big, bad wolf is following you. Or the three little bears."

Justine couldn't help laughing. "You've been reading too many kids' books, Mr. *Forrest*. Your imagination is running wild."

"Indeed."

The way Casson was looking at her made her heart do a flip. Taking a deep breath, she started walking.

If he wanted to walk with her she couldn't very well stop him. And, to be honest, she didn't really want to.

But having him walk so closely beside her was unnerving.

Why did he have to look so gorgeous, even in the moonlight?

Justine shivered, and before she knew it Casson had zipped down his hoodie and taken it off to put it around her shoulders.

Even though she had her own hoodie on, Justine could feel the warmth from his. She couldn't very well take it off and tell him the *real* cause of her shivering.

The fact that her attraction to him was alarming her, especially since the only reason he was at Winter's Haven in the first place was to find a way to convince her to sell.

But, although she might dislike Casson's intentions when it came to her property, she had to admit that there were things about him that she did like. *A lot.* The way he looked, for one. And the way he sounded. The way he cared for Andy.

The way he had come to her rescue and made her feel safe...

Her acknowledgement of liking Casson worried her. How could she even *think* of encouraging any of those feelings? What possible outcome could come from acting on them? After all, Casson would be leaving after his little holiday at Winter's Haven. And she'd still be holding the keys.

"If you're not doing anything tomorrow night..." Casson slackened his pace and waited until she turned to glance at him. "I'd really like to talk to you about my proposal."

Justine's heart plummeted. For a moment it had sounded like he was going to ask her for a date.

Get with it, an inner voice ridiculed. *He wants Winter's Haven, not you. And don't forget it.*

She gave a tired sigh. "I don't really see the purpose of a meeting. There's nothing that would make me contemplate selling. To you or to anyone else."

She picked up her pace, anxious to get home and away from any further discussion around Winter's Haven.

He stepped into place with her. "There are… things I haven't told you," he said softly. "Things that might just change your perspective."

Could he be anymore cryptic?

"If it has to do with offering more money, I'll save you the energy of making the offer." She smiled cynically and tossed her head back. "Not *everyone* can be bought."

"I realize that." He nodded. "I can see how much this place means to you." He reached over as they walked and shifted the hoodie on Justine's shoulders to prevent it from slipping off.

She felt his fingers pause momentarily, and her pulse drummed wildly. And then his hand was off her shoulder. He slowed his pace, and Justine felt like the path leading to her house was an eternity away.

Other than the tread of their footsteps, the chirping of the crickets was the only sound breaking the silence. Justine inhaled the sweet scent of a nearby linden tree.

This is all too much, she thought.

Having Casson walk her home was doing things to her that confused her. She was prepared to battle him verbally, whatever he proposed, and yet her body seemed to want to surrender to him…

Justine stopped walking and frowned. "Why can't you tell me *now*?"

Casson's mouth twisted. "There are things I need to show you as well, and I don't have them with me. Tomorrow we're fishing during the day, so I thought the evening would be a perfect time to—"

Justine practically jumped as Casson's cell phone rang. He reached into his back pocket and a frown appeared on his face.

"Hey, Ronnie, what's up?"

Ronnie's voice came loud and clear. "It's Andy, Cass. His temperature is way up and I'm worried he's going to have a seizure. I need to take him to the hospital…"

"I'm on my way," Casson told her, and stuck his phone back in his pocket. "We'll talk tomorrow," he said to Justine, his hand reaching out to squeeze her arm.

He whistled to Luna, who was investigating a scuttling sound in some bushes. Luna bounded after him and Justine watched with a sick feeling in her stomach as they ran down the driveway and disappeared around the bend.

Casson raced back to the cottage, every footstep matching the beat of his heart. Andy's face and arms were flaming hot. He was moaning, and couldn't keep his eyes open. Ronnie had placed a cool cloth over his forehead and pulled back his top blanket. Casson's heart twisted at the sight of him, and of Ronnie's pale face and wide eyes.

Casson picked Andy up and carefully made his way down the stairs. He set him down gently in the back seat of Ronnie's car while Ronnie sat next to him and fastened his seatbelt before placing a light shawl over him. After a dash inside to make sure there was water in Luna's bowl, Casson drove to the hospital in Parry Sound, hoping he wouldn't get stopped for speeding.

Andy was checked in and seen by midnight. But by the time the doctors had inserted an IV, run some standard tests, and the Emergency Room doctor had examined the results, it was close to four a.m.

Andy was transferred to a room. Although his fever had dropped, the doctors wanted to continue to monitor him, given his condition and recent treatment.

Casson and Ronnie kept vigil by his bedside, taking turns to shut their eyes, and at seven a.m. a doctor came to explain that, although Andy was unlikely to have a seizure, he recommended that a follow-up appointment be made with Andy's specialist at SickKids.

Ronnie decided it was best to take Andy back home and make the appointment.

Casson wanted to drive them home to Gravenhurst, but Ronnie reassured him that she had caught enough sleep to handle the drive alone.

With her reassurance that she would call him if she needed him, Casson brushed a kiss on Andy's forehead and they left the hospital.

By the time he drove her car back to the cottage, and she returned to the hospital they would be ready to discharge Andy.

When Casson got out of Ronnie's car and she switched to the driver's seat he reached down to give her a hug. "Drive safely, Ronnie. And call me when you get home."

Casson watched her drive away, then entered the cottage to Luna's welcome. He opened the door to let her run out, and when they were both inside again took off his shoes and, without bothering to undress, fell on top of his bed and crashed.

Casson woke up three hours later. He felt pretty ragged, and could only imagine how Ronnie felt. He checked his phone and saw that Ronnie had texted to say they were home and she would let him know of any developments with Andy. He sent her a quick message, apologizing for sleeping through the text and sending them hugs.

He not only felt rough, he looked it, too, he thought a few moments later, staring at his reflection in the bathroom mirror. He stroked his jaw and chin. He had let his usual five o'clock shadow grow for over two weeks, and now he decided the scruff had to go.

After shaving he had a hot shower, letting the pulsating jets ease the tension in his muscles. He lathered himself with the shower gel provided, his nose wrinkling at the scent. It reminded him of something…of *Justine,* he realized.

He glanced at the label. Rose Rapture. Wonderful, he thought wryly, rinsing off, he'd always wanted to come out smelling like a rose. Stepping out of the shower, he grabbed a towel and briskly dried himself. Wrapping it around his hips, and stepping into flip-flops, he padded into the kitchen and put the coffee on.

Casson reached into the cupboard to get a mug, and then a movement at the screen door caught his eye. He stood there, mug in hand, towel around his hips, and met Justine's embarrassed gaze through the glass of the door.

CHAPTER FOURTEEN

JUSTINE HAD BEEN on the verge of turning away, but now it was too late. Casson had already seen her. She let her hand drop, wishing she had thought to call first. He didn't seem too perturbed over the fact that he was wearing nothing but a towel, though, and she tried to keep her eyes from wandering as he walked to the door. She focused on his face, now clean-shaven, and couldn't help but gulp.

Shadow or no shadow, Casson was gorgeous. Drop-dead gorgeous.

He opened the door and she blurted, "Is Andy okay? Is he back from the hospital? I made some chicken soup for him and some lemon blueberry muffins…" She stopped, and looked down at the stainless steel pot she was holding on to for dear life, aware that she was blabbering.

"That's very kind of you, Justine." Casson smiled. "His fever dropped, thank goodness.

They checked him out…did some tests. He might just have been overtired, and with his compromised immune system it doesn't take much to knock him down. The doctor suggested Ronnie do a follow-up at SickKids. They're home now. Come in," he added, taking the pot and container.

The sight of his sculpted torso sent a ripple of pure desire through her body. As he set the items down on the kitchen counter she felt her cheeks burning. She patted Luna and then turned around slowly, hoping Casson had gone to change, but he was still standing across from her, one hand on the back of a chair and the other on his hip.

"I suppose I should go and get decent," he said, the corners of his mouth lifting. "I'll be right back."

"Um…well, since Ronnie and Andy aren't here you can have the soup and muffins yourself…" Justine said, trying hard to keep her eyes on his face.

"I don't think so," he drawled, his eyes crinkling at the corners. "We can have the muffins with coffee. As for the soup—we can share it later. If you haven't already made supper plans."

He started to walk away, and then paused to look back at her.

"Since you're here now, we might as well have that meeting I was talking about yesterday. But I think you'll be much more receptive to what I have to tell you if I put some clothes on." He grinned. "It's so much more professional than just wearing a towel and Rose Rapture."

Justine felt her cheeks flaming. She couldn't tear her gaze away from him as he strode away, and her eyes took in every detail from his damp, curling dark hair to his muscled neck and sculpted arms and shoulders. And the firm slope to the small of his back…

As the door clicked shut Justine snapped out of her stupor and took a deep breath. She wiped her brow. It was a hot one today, but she felt even hotter inside—especially after seeing Casson half naked. Again, she wished she had thought to phone him instead of just showing up at his door…

She wondered what exactly he had to show her. He seemed to think it could sway her in some way. She couldn't help feeling apprehensive. Too much had happened since Casson had set foot at

Winter's Haven, and somehow she had an uneasy feeling that he had something up his sleeve. Something that might tip the scales in his favor.

Justine braced herself. She had no intention of letting him weaken her resolve. No matter what he presented her with, she would turn it down.

"Hey, make yourself at home." Casson chuckled, coming out of his room with a large brown envelope in his hand. He had changed into a black T-shirt and a pair of faded jeans with a couple of worn-through spots above the knees.

Justine wished he didn't have to look so damned sexy. She pulled out a chair at the kitchen table and sat down while Casson poured coffee into two mugs. He set out the milk and then, sitting down across from her, helped himself to a muffin.

"Mmm." He nodded. "Thanks for breakfast." He pushed the container toward her.

"I had one earlier, thanks."

She stared pointedly at the envelope beside him. Casson had tried to hand her this very envelope before, when he had first come to her house. He had said it was a development proposal drafted by an architect friend of his, and had suggested that she at least give the plan and drawings a glance. He obviously thought that whatever was in the envelope might dispel her doubts about his venture.

Well, she still had doubts. Only she supposed she could let him at least show her his plans.

Casson set his mug down. “Look, Justine, do you have plans this afternoon?”

“Wh-why?” Justine shifted uncomfortably.

“It might take some time to go over the details.”

“I can’t imagine there will be much to discuss,” she said, “so don’t get your hopes up.” She didn’t want Casson to think that there was even the *slightest* chance she would change her mind about selling.

His eyes blazed into hers and his mouth curved slightly. “A man can always hope,” he drawled. “Well?”

“Well, what?” She tossed her head.

“*Are* you free this afternoon?”

“I will be after you show me what’s in the envelope. I’ll have a few minutes. But then I have to run a quick errand before relieving Mandy. She’s off early today to go to a wedding.”

"Mmm..." Casson rubbed his chin. "I need more than a few minutes." He tapped his fingers on the table top. "Why don't we leave the envelope till later this evening? Do you have time to go out for lunch? My treat." He smiled crookedly. "To thank you for your kindness to Andy."

Justine felt a slow flush creep over her cheeks. "That's not necessary."

"Look, Justine..." He set his elbows on the table and leaned closer, his gaze becoming serious. "A lot has happened for both of us in the last couple of days. Let's forget about the sale and everything else for a while and just enjoy an hour. Away from work, away from worry. What do you say?" His eyebrows lifted.

Justine examined his face for the slightest sign of insincerity and couldn't find one. She glanced at the time on her phone. "I'm sorry. I don't even have an hour."

Darn, if only she had brought the soup over earlier...

"Thanks for the offer, though."

Flushing, Justine averted her gaze and patted Luna before leaving. She resisted the temptation of looking back as she walked toward her car.

As she pulled out of the driveway she glanced in her rearview mirror. Casson was in the doorway, watching her…

Casson rubbed his chin as Justine drove off. He was disappointed that his impromptu offer hadn't worked out, but there was still tonight to look forward to.

Justine's expression when she'd told him not to get his hopes up had been so different from when she'd had first arrived at the door, when she'd tried not to show that she was glancing at his body… He had caught a spark of *something* in those blue-gray depths then. Something that made him wonder if there was a current below the surface, a fuse that just needed to be lit.

No matter how much Justine tried to show otherwise, Casson felt deep in his gut that she wasn't immune to him. Maybe at first, when she'd fallen into his lap and they'd kissed, it might have been just physical for both of them, but after their evening around the campfire he'd sensed there was something *deeper*. He had *felt* it. It had been as if she were seeing him with new eyes.

He had caught her expression when he was

with Andy, too; it had seemed softer, relaxed, approving. But of course there was a limit to her approval. She was far from approving of his intentions regarding Winter's Haven.

But maybe that would change tonight.

His initial plan was to show her the architect's drawings and then suggest she sell him Winter's Haven with the proviso that she would manage his new resort. If she accepted his offer he would agree to delay renovations or construction until he had a deeper understanding of the unique features of the huge parcel of land that comprised both the Russell properties and Winter's Haven.

Justine would be a great asset, and he was sure that eventually she would see that what he was planning would not be to the detriment of the landscape, but an enhancement—with the most important consequence being its benefit to kids like Andy, and their parent or parents, who deserved some pampering after dealing with the heartbreak of a cancer diagnosis and treatment for their child.

And then he would show her the deed.

She would be shocked, perhaps even angry, but it had to be done. Justine had the right to know.

And maybe the knowledge that he owned part of Winter's Haven already might just sway her into considering selling…

If Justine still balked after that he would pull out his ace: a considerable increase in his initial price offer and, if she agreed to it, an offer for her to continue to live in the house rent-free for as long as she was managing Franklin's Resort.

Casson closed the door. It was too bad their fishing trip today was a bust. Andy would have loved it. He checked the time on his cell phone and wondered how Andy was doing. His stomach twisted at the memory of Andy moaning, his face contorted and pale.

Grabbing his phone, he sent Ronnie a text.

Ronnie responded quickly, saying that Andy was resting and his temperature had stabilized. She thanked him for everything and promised to visit him again when Andy got the go-ahead from his specialist in Toronto.

The pot sitting on the counter caught his eye. The chicken soup Justine had made for a sick little boy she hardly knew.

His heart swelled.

She's a keeper, an inner voice told him as he placed the pot in the fridge.

"Time for a swim," he called out to Luna, and she bounded after him.

He could do with a splash in the bay.

Afterwards, Casson stretched out on a chaise lounge, and Luna plunked herself down next to him. He reached out and stroked her back. Much as he loved his dog, he thought about how nice it would be to have Justine lying next to him…

He propped himself on his side and looked out at the bay, a blue sheet twinkling with diamonds under the sunny sky. He could hardly believe that in two days his Franklin & Casson on the Bay exhibition would open.

Before he'd left home to take possession of the Russells' properties he had checked with all his contacts to ensure that everything was in place for the event. The paintings would be kept in a secure depository until the day before the opening. Lighting was adjusted. Security was arranged. Responses from the invited patrons verified. Media presence confirmed. An adjoining room had been prepared for the silent auction. The banquet courses were finalized.

All this had been delegated to a committee he had carefully chosen almost a year earlier. They were all prepared, as was he.

There was only one thing he hadn't planned or even considered up to now…and that was bringing a date.

CHAPTER FIFTEEN

JUSTINE LOOKED UP to see Mandy walking toward her. She hadn't even heard her car in the driveway.

"Nice cut and style," she said. "But what are you doing back here?"

"I left the wedding card on the desk. Here it is." Mandy peered at her with a slight frown. "Hey, why did you look so glum when I first walked in? Like you lost your best friend…"

Justine sighed and told her about Andy and his illness, and how Casson and Ronnie had rushed him to the hospital…

"Poor little fellow," Mandy said. "I hope it turns out to be nothing serious…" She sat on a corner of the desk. "My goodness, there seems to be a lot of drama around Casson Forrester. And not only at Winter's Haven."

"What do you mean?" Justine frowned.

"While I was waiting for my hairdresser to call

me over I checked out the public bulletin board. There was a poster about an event that Casson's putting on at the Stockey Centre. It's being sponsored by his company, Forrest Hardware. I can't believe neither of us heard about it before."

"What kind of event? A home show?"

Mandy chuckled. "No, it has nothing to do with lumber or building. It's an art exhibition—two of the Group of Seven artists. Some of their most famous works will be on display for a week, and there's also a silent auction for one of the paintings on opening night, and an invitation-only fund-raising banquet."

Justine's mind raced.

Casson had never mentioned an exhibition when he was telling her about the Franklin painting...or had she forgotten?

No, she wouldn't have forgotten something like that.

And why hadn't he mentioned it at all today?

"When is this happening?" Justine tried to keep her voice steady, thinking about Casson's brother and his connection with *Mirror Lake.*

"All next week. Why? Do you want to go?" Mandy raised her eyebrows. "It starts on Monday night. Two days from now." She sighed dramatically. "I can't believe this guy. Not only is he gorgeous and successful—oh, and did I mention gorgeous?" She laughed. "He's also a devoted godfather *and* a patron of the arts. I've checked all the boxes under 'Man of Your Dreams.' She glanced slyly at Justine. "Except maybe the categories of 'great cook' and 'even better lover.'"

Justine's mouth dropped open. "Are you *kidding* me?"

"I'm serious. He's single, you're single, and now that you've found out that Ronnie's his cousin you should grab your chance while he's on your property, for heaven's sakes." She gave Justine's shoulder a gentle punch. "I think you'd make a great couple."

"I think it takes a little more than *that* to make a couple, Mandy," she scoffed, returning the soft punch. "And, besides, he wants my property—not *me.*"

Mandy walked away, shrugging.

Before the door closed behind her Justine called out sheepishly, "What did you say the name of the event was?"

"Franklin & Casson on the Bay."

* * *

Later, after closing the office, Justine went home and changed into a sky blue bikini. It was too humid to do anything but go for a refreshing swim.

Walking down to the beach, Justine couldn't stop thinking about Casson. About his exhibition and what he had told her about his brother Franklin, and what he *hadn't* told her. The fact that he was a patron of the arts just added to the data she had been unconsciously accumulating about him from the time he had stepped foot on her property.

There was quite an accumulation of physical data. She had to admit that when she wasn't involved with desk matters or the cottagers at Winter's Haven her brain kept summoning up images of Casson. They flicked through her memory as if she were looking through a photo gallery online: Casson in a tailored suit, his dark chestnut eyes glinting at her; Casson sitting in his Mustang convertible; Casson by the campfire and Casson walking through the door with a towel around his hips. Images that circulated constantly in her head.

The emotional data took up just as much space. The knowledge of his relationship with his brother. His congenial manner with Mandy and Melody and the cottagers in the diner. His kindness and caring toward Andy and Ronnie. His love for his dog. His appreciation for art. His entrepreneurial drive and success in building the Forrest Hardware chain.

But there was so much more that she wanted to know…

What had she filled her thoughts with before Casson walked into her life?

Whoa, there, she chided herself. He had walked onto her property, not into her *life*.

That realization sobered her. Besides his showing a typical male physical reaction to her on occasion, she couldn't delude herself into thinking that Casson Forrester had any emotional intentions or feelings toward her. Sure, he had shown some consideration, even kindness and concern, but…

But what? an inner voice prompted.

But she wanted more.

Justine bit her lip. Yes, she couldn't deny it to herself any longer. Casson had sparked something within her, and she couldn't control what it was igniting throughout her entire being—not only physically, but emotionally as well. She wanted *him.* Despite all her conflicting feelings about his ploys to get her to sell, she wanted Casson to want *her* more than he wanted Winter's Haven.

But it wasn't that simple.

Or was it?

The sudden urge to go and see Casson stopped Justine in her tracks. He *had* mentioned something about sharing the chicken soup…

She ran back up to the house, slipped on a pair of yellow cotton shorts and a shirt patterned with yellow daisies over her bikini.

Maybe she needed to *show* Casson Forrester that she was interested. Besides throwing herself into his arms—which was what she wished she could do—she had to come up with *something* to see if he was interested too.

And then maybe eventually she'd have the nerve to reveal the fact that she was falling in love with him.

Casson thought about going to the diner before supper. The swim in the bay had revitalized him, and he wanted to chat with the other cottagers and get a feel for what they liked about Winter's Haven and the area. This was his opportunity to discover what features to keep and what could be changed or added in future.

If Justine sold to him.

This last thought jolted him. Before, he had always thought in terms of *when* Justine sold to him.

Why the sudden uncertainty?

He brushed off any remaining beach sand from his feet and Luna's fur, hung his towel to dry on the outside line and entered the cottage. His gaze settled on the pot on the counter. Maybe he should scrap his idea about going to the diner now in case Justine decided to come over a little early…

While Luna was happily devouring her supper Casson went to his room and changed into a white T-shirt and khaki shorts. Whistling, he returned to the kitchen to check the soup, the aroma making his mouth water. He heard his phone ring from his bedroom and sprinted to get it, expecting it to be Ronnie.

His stomach twisted with the thought that

Andy's condition might have worsened. But his phone didn't show any caller ID. He frowned.

"Hello?"

"Hello, this is Justine..."

Casson's stomach did a flip. "Hi."

"I—I thought I'd give you a call before coming to knock at your door," she said. "I have some time if you want to show me whatever it is you have to show me..."

Yes!

"Oh, well, a call wasn't necessary. You could have just come to the door."

He heard her clearing her throat. "Well... I just wanted to make sure you were...you weren't..."

He suddenly got it. She didn't want to come unannounced to the door and find him half-undressed again. The thought made him want to laugh, but he restrained himself.

"I'm fully clothed and I'm just heating up your soup," he said. "I was hoping you'd join me."

"Okay... I wouldn't want it to go to waste. And then we can talk."

"Are you at the office? When can you get away?"

"I'm at the end of your driveway," Justine said,

and Casson detected a note of sheepishness in her voice. "I'll be there in a minute."

Casson looked out the kitchen window and there she was, straddling her bike as she paused to phone him. He saw her putting her phone in her pocket and start to pedal toward the cottage.

His smile turned into a grin before he burst out laughing.

Casson was holding the door open for her. Justine smiled her thanks and started to walk by him, but Luna's rush to the door stopped her in her tracks. She was penned in between Luna and Casson, who had now shut the door and was standing directly behind her.

"Hey, girl." Justine bent to pat Luna and then immediately regretted it, when her backside brushed against Casson's body. She straightened instantly, her face flaming, and was glad she couldn't see Casson's expression.

"Luna,—couch," Casson's amused voice drawled behind her, and Luna gave a plaintive howl but proceeded to obey.

Justine wiped her brow with her forearm. The humidity outside was high, but it was stifling in the cottage. She wished she could just strip off her clothes and remain in her bikini, like she did in her own house.

She glanced at him edgewise as he set the table. If he'd looked gorgeous in a black T-shirt, he looked magnificent in the white one he was wearing now. It emphasized his broad shoulders, and the firm contours of his chest and stomach. And his khaki shorts fit him oh, so well…

Justine couldn't help thinking that he looked like a hunky model out of a magazine.

Casson put a bottle of white wine in the fridge and then set the platter of cheese and crackers on the table.

"I suppose I should have thought of bringing something a little cooler," Justine said as Casson filled two bowls with soup, "but I thought if Andy was sick chicken soup would do him good."

"Your intentions were honorable," Casson said, and smiled, "and that's what counts."

Justine felt her insides quiver as she met his warm gaze.

They ate in silence for a few minutes and then Casson suddenly rose from his chair. "What am

I thinking?" His eyes glinted. "There's cheese, but no wine on the table. Forgive me, my lady."

He gave a mock bow. A spiral of pleasure danced through Justine's body at his words. If only he knew how much she wanted to be *his lady.*

He poured white wine into two glasses and offered her one. "Let's toast our little Andy's health."

They clinked glasses and Justine's gaze locked with Casson's as she tasted the wine—a Pinot Grigio from Niagara-on-the-Lake. With its peachy bouquet and hint of vanilla, it complemented the Oka and the other cheeses Casson had selected.

"Let's take it down to the beach," he said suddenly, when they had each finished their first glass. "It's too hot in the cottage. I'll bring the wine and the glasses, and you can bring the cheese tray." He laughed. "Luna can bring herself."

Justine couldn't quite believe what was happening. Earlier she had decided to show Casson that she was interested. Now here she was, following this gorgeous man to a private beach where they would be sharing wine and cheese on the most sultry night of the summer.

She shivered in anticipation, the wine in her system already starting to loosen her up.

They sat side by side in the Muskoka chairs, nibbling on cheese and crackers and cooling themselves with wine. There was no breeze whatsoever, and the surface of the bay was mirror-still. In minutes it would be dusk, and Justine's pulse quickened at the thought of being with Casson in the darkness.

The sky was a magnificent palette in the twilight, with streaks of vermillion, orange, magenta and gold. She turned to Casson, exclaiming at the beauty of it, and met his intense gaze.

He held out his glass. "Here's to another beauty," he said huskily, and leaned over so that his face was close to hers.

Their glasses clinked but neither of them drank. Casson moved closer, and with a pulsating in her chest that spread down her body Justine felt herself tilting her face so his lips could meet hers. When they made contact, ever so lightly, Justine closed her eyes with the wonder of it. And when Casson's lips pressed against hers, and then moved over her bottom lip, she thought her limbs would melt.

She let out a small gasp, giving Casson the opportunity to deepen the kiss. She was sure her heart would explode as she reciprocated, tasting the wine on his tongue.

Justine lost all sense of time and space, and when he finally released her the glorious colors of the sky had faded to dusky gray and indigo. He took her hand and helped her stand up. Pulling her to him, he lifted his hands to cup the back of her head and kissed her again.

Justine wrapped her arms around his waist, then slid them up his back and around his neck. She trembled when his hands began their descent down her back and around her waist, before finding the edge of her cotton top. And then his hands were on her bare waist, searing her already heated skin.

"Let's go for a dip," he said, his breath ragged.

He pulled off his shirt and tossed it on a chair. He left his khaki shorts on. She let him help her pull off her top and shorts, and was thrilled at the way his eyes blazed when his fingers brushed against her bikini top and bottom.

Somewhere in the distance a loon gave its haunting call, and as they splashed their way into the still but bracingly cold depths of the bay, with Luna following, Justine felt freer than she had ever felt in her life.

After the initial shock of the water on their heated skin they automatically came together. The water was up to Justine's chest. Justine tilted her head back as Casson's lips traced a path up her neck to her mouth. He pulled her in even closer, and their bodies fit together in a way that sent a series of jolts through her.

As Casson's hands began to wander over the thin material of her bikini Justine gasped in pleasure at the sensation under water. She let her hands wander as well, sliding over the firm expanse of his back, exploring his contours. She kissed the base of his neck and his mouth, giving in to the desires that had been simmering within her and needing release for days.

Casson was in another world, with Justine pressed against him in the water, his senses filled with the sight and feel of her. He wanted to stroke every part of her with his hands and his lips, to make her gasp with pleasure. She looked like a sea nymph, with those smoldering blue eyes and silky skin. She was looking up at him now, their bodies locked together, their arms encircling each other.

The dark sky was suddenly lit up with a flash of lightning and the effect was surreal, the light reflecting in each other's eyes.

Luna started barking. She had already dashed out of the water after a quick dip, and had been waiting for them on the beach, but now she was running about in a panic from the electricity in the air. When the rolls of thunder followed she started yelping even more, and ran frantically in and out of the water.

The rain started seconds later.

Casson took Justine's hand, and by the time they got out of the water and onto the beach the rain was pelting down on them. It was warm rain, but heavy, falling down in sheets. They quickly gathered their clothes, and the items they had left by the Muskoka chairs and table, and dashed to the cottage.

Once inside, they stood in the entrance, the rain dripping off their bodies onto the linoleum floor.

"Luna—stay." Casson patted her, trying to calm her. "Lie down, girl."

He turned to Justine and his heart thumped at the sight of her standing there, barefoot in her bikini, her drenched hair clinging to her cheeks, her dusky blue eyes wide and fluttering, her eyelashes beaded with raindrops. Despite the warmth inside the cottage, she had started to shiver.

He put his hands on her shoulders. "Don't move," he murmured. "I'm going to grab some towels."

He leaned over and planted a kiss on her lips. He had to tear himself away then, before his prehistoric instincts took over and he picked her up, dripping and all, and carried her straight into his man cave.

He brought back three bath towels. He placed one over Justine's shoulders and set one aside while he ran the third towel over Luna and wiped the beach sand from her paws.

"Okay, Luna, go on your mat."

He turned to Justine. She was towel-drying her hair. Gently he took the towel out of her hands and continued to pat her hair dry. Then he proceeded to dry her neck, her shoulders and back, before moving to the front of her body. He held her gaze with his as he patted her chest and moved downward. By the time he reached her thighs and calves he could feel shivers running through him—although he suspected it had nothing to do with being cold.

"Here..." Justine took the towel from him and hung it on a hook behind the door. She reached for the remaining dry towel and wrapped it around his head. "My turn." She smiled shyly and started drying his hair. And then she followed his lead, slowly patting him dry, lingering in some areas more than others...

She made him catch his breath, and her eyes seemed to flash in delight at his reaction to her touch. When she was done they stood there, staring into each other's eyes, and he suddenly knew, without a doubt, that Justine had completely snagged him.

Hook, line and sinker.

CHAPTER SIXTEEN

JUSTINE PRACTICALLY JUMPED into Casson's arms at the next crack of thunder. Luna gave a howl and started to tear around the cottage, panting and giving low growls.

"You can't go home in this weather," Casson said, drawing Justine closer.

"You could drive me," she murmured, sounding unconvincing even to herself.

"I couldn't leave Luna alone; she'd be terrified," Casson said, sounding relieved that he had come up with an excuse. "You can have my room. I'll sleep on the couch. Luna will want me near her tonight."

Justine stopped herself from blurting out, *So will I.*

She took a deep breath. Things were spinning away too fast for her. *She* was spinning. She needed some space, some distance to make sense of what was happening between her and Casson.

And spending the night in the same cottage with him, even if they were in separate rooms, would provide her with neither enough space nor distance.

"You should get out of your wet bikini," Casson said "I'll go get you some of my clothes." He chuckled. "I'll see what I can find in your size."

While he went to his room Justine went to comfort Luna. It felt so strange, walking around barefoot in a bikini *here*. Her stomach fluttered with the prospect of sleeping in Casson's bed. Could she trust him to stay on the couch?

Could she trust herself...?

Casson came out of the bedroom with a navy T-shirt. "This will have to do," he said, and held it out to Justine. "You can change in here."

Justine felt herself flushing. The T-shirt was large, and would probably reach her knees. *But she wouldn't be wearing anything underneath.* And of course it wouldn't cross Casson's mind to offer her a pair of his shorts.

She took the T-shirt from him and went into his room, shutting the door firmly behind her. She took deep breaths to slow down the beating of her heart. Scanning the room, she wasn't surprised to see how neat and orderly it was. Bed made, clothes hung up in the partially open wardrobe, and a suitcase in one corner of the room. Her eyes fell on the open laptop on the desk, and she saw the brown envelope he had brought out earlier.

She walked over to the bed and set the T-shirt on it while she took off her bikini. She caught sight of herself in the dresser mirror and felt her pulse leaping at the thought of Casson seeing her this way. She shivered and slipped the T-shirt on. It came to just above her knees, and it was baggy, but at least it was dry.

She still felt vulnerable, though, and had the crazy thought of searching through the drawers in the night table for a pair of his underwear. She sat on the bed, considering it, and saw a bottle of Casson's cologne on the night table.

Unable to resist, she picked it up. She uncapped it and inhaled the scent she had come to recognize: a blend of bamboo, pine and musk. An expensive Italian brand she had seen advertised in magazines.

A sudden thumping noise at the bedroom door startled her, and she fumbled with the bottle. She caught it before it could fall and break on the plank floor, but in grabbing it she accidentally sprayed herself.

Cursing inwardly, she set the bottle back on the night table. *Explain that to Casson...*

"Luna, get away from that door," she heard Casson say, chuckling. "Your friend is coming out any minute."

When Justine opened the door she saw Casson's eyes scanning over her appreciatively. He walked toward her and stopped, his nose wrinkling.

Justine smiled sheepishly. "Accident," she murmured, shrugging.

He leaned over and sniffed deeply, his nose and lips grazing her neck. She couldn't help shivering as he released his breath, and the sensation on her skin made her heart begin to pound.

"I guess I won't have to put any cologne on, then," he said huskily. "I'll go and change, too." He gazed at the bikini top and bottom in her hand, and then back at her. "You can hang those and your other clothes in the washroom."

When Justine returned to the living room she sat on the edge of the couch, her stomach in knots as she waited for Casson to come. She would tell him she was exhausted and would be going to bed right away, she decided.

A moment later he emerged, wearing blue-striped pajama bottoms and a beige T-shirt, holding a pillow in one hand and a change of clothes in the other. Justine's heart flipped. She stood up, knowing she'd better get to his room before…before her resolve started to weaken.

"I'm beat," she said. "I'll say goodnight."

She gave him a half-smile and quickly averted her gaze. She patted Luna, then gingerly stepped past Casson. To her relief he didn't stop her, and as she closed the bedroom door with a click she let out her breath.

She left the wooden shutters in his room partially open, so the morning light would wake her, and then turned off the light switch. As she slipped into bed she began to have second doubts.

Was she crazy? Passing up an opportunity to spend the night with Casson in this bed?

He would be beside her right now had she given him the slightest indication of wanting that.

Justine bit her lip. She had come to his cottage with the intention of showing him that she was interested and seeing if he felt the same. Well, she had no doubts that he was interested in her body—neither of them could deny the chemistry between them. But she wanted—no, *needed*—more than that. She needed to know that Casson Forrester wanted her heart and soul as well. When she knew that for sure, *then* she would be his.

She snuggled under the covers, savoring the feeling of intimacy in just lying on the sheet Casson slept on. She breathed in his scent on the pillow, and let it and the rhythm of the rain, and the muted grumbling of thunder, soothe her to sleep.

Casson stared at the door for a few moments after Justine had closed it. Tonight was going to be sweet torture, lying on the couch. How could he possibly sleep, knowing that Justine was only steps away? Especially after the intimacy they had shared?

He groaned softly and, turning off the kitchen light, made his way to the couch. He plunked down his pillow and stretched out. It was too humid in the cottage to cover up. And too hot for pajamas. He pulled them off impatiently, leaving his boxers on. With any luck he'd get a breeze coming through the screened-in windows during the night.

Good luck falling asleep.

Casson felt so frustrated. And deflated. Justine had relayed her intentions loud and clear after he had given her his T-shirt. *I'm beat. I'll say goodnight.* He couldn't deny it: if he had seen even a spark in Justine's eye to invite him to follow her into the bedroom he wouldn't have thought twice. But she had deliberately avoided looking at him.

Although he had seen her blue eyes darken with desire in the bay, and when they were drying each other, something had caused Justine to pull back. Could she still have feelings for Robert? *No!* He didn't want to believe that. His jaw tensed. Or maybe Justine's suspicions about his intentions had resurfaced, making her keep any attraction she felt for him in check, especially after her experience with Robert. Maybe she believed he was using her, trying to use sex to influence her decision not to sell.

She didn't trust him.

Casson felt as if someone had kicked him in the gut. He breathed in deeply and exhaled slowly.

He wanted Justine to trust him, to believe that he wasn't using her.

But how could he convince her of that? Convince her that it wasn't just her body he had fallen in love with, but her gentle spirit?

Yes, he thought in wonder, *he had fallen in love with her.*

She was kind and considerate…making soup for a little boy she hardly knew. And it wasn't because she had some ulterior motive to get Casson to like her. No, it was simply a thoughtful and sensitive gesture. And she was kind to Luna. Casson had seen a flash of real sorrow in her eyes when he'd told her about how Luna had been abandoned and left at the side of the road. And what about her concern that Robert would be ruined if they'd called the police? It was only because of her that Casson hadn't gone down that route. *He* would have been much harder on Robert. And he really hadn't expected Justine to demonstrate that kind of compassion after Robert's behavior.

But Justine was soft. *Softer.* And that was what he loved about her. She had a gentleness and a generosity that his previous dates had lacked. He might have been too focused on building his business to spend time searching for the right person in his life, but now Casson realized that a search was not necessary.

He closed his eyes and turned onto one side. He felt drained. So much had happened since that first meeting with Justine. He let some of the memories play in his mind for a while, but then, remembering that tomorrow evening was the opening of the Franklin & Casson on the Bay exhibition, he pushed those thoughts back.

He had checked his email earlier, and everything was ready to go at the Stockey Centre. The banner stands were in place, the paintings were arranged, the lighting adjusted. And the A. J. Casson painting was sitting regally on an antique brass easel next to the mahogany desk in the silent auction room.

The media would arrive at five-thirty p.m. to interview Casson and local dignitaries. The doors would open to the public at six. Casson would make a formal address at six-thirty, sharing his vision of Franklin's Resort before unveiling the A. J. Casson painting.

He had arranged the hiring of two notable gallery owners, who were experts on the Group of Seven—especially the two featured artists—to interact with the public and enlighten them about the individual paintings on display. Casson would also mingle with the invited patrons and the public.

At seven, the invited guests would make their way to the banquet room, where they would enjoy a fabulous five-course meal. The event would close at nine o'clock.

Casson felt a twinge in his heart. The three banner stands he had ordered showed an enlarged photo of him and Franklin at their parents' friends' cottage in Georgian Bay. The title was at the top: Franklin & Casson on the Bay. One would be placed in the entrance of the Stockey Centre, another would be in the exhibition room, and the third would be in the room displaying the A. J. Casson painting for the silent auction.

The photo had been taken by his mother, in the summer two months before Franklin's diagnosis. He and Franklin were standing on the dock, the bay a brilliant blue behind them, and he was helping Franklin hold up his fishing rod. The fish—a pickerel—wasn't big, but it was a keeper.

The backs of Casson's eyes started to sting. He squeezed them shut and turned his pillow over.

Okay, Franklin, tomorrow evening's the big event. Get some sleep up there in heaven, buddy, 'cause you're coming with me, and it'll be past your bedtime when we're done.

CHAPTER SEVENTEEN

JUSTINE SCREAMED, AND seconds later her eyes fluttered open. She sat up, her back against the headboard, and then, her heart thudding, she heard the door clicking open. The light came on to reveal that it was Casson.

He turned the dimmer switch on low and closed the door behind him. He strode to the foot of the bed. "Are you okay? Did you have a bad dream?"

Justine felt her lip quivering.

The nightmare had seemed so real.

Casson had been walking her home, and they had arrived at the edge of her property when she'd caught sight of a wrecking ball, advancing toward her house. She'd started to scream, and Casson had tried to silence her with a kiss. She'd managed to pull away and had screamed again as one side of her house had caved in.

And then she'd woken up.

Justine blinked. The genuine concern in Casson's eyes pushed her emotions over the edge. She felt her eyes filling up and, biting her lip, nodded. "I—I was dreaming that—that you were starting to have my house torn down so you could build your resort…"

She shivered and burst into tears, covering her face with her hands. Then sucked in her breath when she felt a shift in the mattress and Casson's arms around her. She didn't have the strength to move away from the warmth of his embrace. She felt herself sinking against his chest, and as he held her tightly she let the tears flow.

How could she have such conflicting feelings about Casson? Her wariness about his motives concerning Winter's Haven was manifesting itself even in her dreams, and yet she couldn't deny or resist his magnetic pull.

"It's okay, Justine," he murmured, gently stroking the back of her head. "I would never have your home demolished; I can promise you that."

His heartbeat seemed to leap up to her ear, and for a few seconds she just concentrated on its rhythm while inhaling the heady pine scent of his cologne.

"I'm sorry," she whispered, moving her face

away from the wet spot on his T-shirt. "I—I didn't mean to slobber all over you."

She looked up and met his gaze tremulously. His expression made her heart flip.

Slowly his hand slid from the back of her head to cup her chin. He held it there, and with his other hand slowly wiped the tears from her cheeks. His fingers fanned her face gently, and she felt an exquisite swirling in her stomach at his tenderness. When he leaned closer she stopped breathing, and when his lips kissed her forehead she blew out a long, slow breath and closed her eyes.

"Oh, Cass..."

His lips continued to trace a path over each eye, the bridge of her nose and her cheeks, before finding the lobe of her ear. There his mouth lingered, opening to catch the tip in his mouth. She drew in her breath sharply and a flame of arousal shot through her like the fuse on an explosive. By the time his lips made their way to her mouth her lips were parted and her whole body was trembling in anticipation.

His lips closed over her upper lip and then her lower one, pressing, tasting, before exploring deeper. Justine let out a small moan and felt herself surrendering, her senses flooded with the taste, smell and feel of him. Her body and his seemed to move in synchronicity, and in seconds the bedcovers were off and they were entwined on the mattress.

Casson pressed her against him and she wrapped her arms around his back, reveling in the heat and hardness of his body.

Justine knew there was no going back when Casson's lips started tracing a path from her neck downward. She shivered when he lifted her T-shirt off, wanting to squirm as his gaze devoured her. Casson shifted to one side and in two quick movements his own clothes were off.

With a searing desire she had never felt before Justine extended her arms and Casson gave himself to her.

At the first light of dawn Casson woke up. He stretched languorously before easing himself off the couch. His body tingled with the memory of his lovemaking with Justine. After they had both been sated they had dozed off. Hours later, when Luna had started pawing at the door and whimpering, Casson had returned to the couch, not wanting to disturb Justine. Besides, he'd needed to be up early to prepare for opening night.

If he hadn't had the exhibition to host this evening he would have been happy to nestle in Justine's arms all day…but the reality was he had to drive back home to Huntsville, get his suit and shoes for the event, and exchange his Mustang for the Ferrari.

There was no way he'd be going to the opening gala without it. and with Franklin's ball cap on the seat next to him. Then he'd go back to the cottage, and hopefully he'd see Justine before heading to the Stockey Centre.

He decided it would be better to leave Luna there, for when Justine woke up. He glanced at his bedroom door. He had left his laptop in his room but, much as he wanted to, he couldn't bring himself to go in. He checked for new messages on his phone instead and then, satisfied that his committee had everything in place, changed into jeans and a shirt.

Casson started as Luna pawed at the front door. He opened the door as quietly as he could and when they'd returned prepared Luna's dish and set it down.

"Now, you be a good girl until I get back, Luna. Shh…no noise."

He gave her an affectionate scratch behind the ears and then started to walk to the door. Suddenly his footsteps slowed and he abruptly turned around.

What am I doing? I need to let Justine know about the event…

Casson had thought about telling Justine about it a few times before, but had always changed his mind, waiting for the right time to enlighten her as to the real reason for his resort venture.

Well, it was now or never…

Taking a strip of paper off a notepad, Casson scribbled a note to Justine and left it on the table. She might be furious with him for arranging such an event before even securing Winter's Haven, but he was willing to risk her wrath by having her come to the Stockey Centre and learn the real reason behind his actions.

Maybe then she would have a change of heart.

And if she was still absolutely against selling

Winter's Haven he would go ahead and make her a new offer.

She could keep Winter's Haven and he would develop only the Russell properties for his venture, with her as manager.

It would be on a much smaller scale than he had originally planned, but he was willing to make some changes if that would keep Justine happy. And *he* would be happy having Justine as manager.

Who was he kidding?

It wasn't just that he wanted a manager. He wanted the love of a woman.

One woman... Justine.

He finished the note, turned the coffee maker on, and then slipped quietly out the door.

CHAPTER EIGHTEEN

THE AROMA OF coffee tingled Justine's nostrils and she opened her eyes, disoriented. It took her a few seconds to realize that she wasn't in her own room. Turning her head to look around, she felt it all come flooding back to her.

She was in Casson's bed.

She had gone to bed in here and he had gone to sleep on the couch.

Her eyes widened at the onrush of memories…

She had screamed, and Casson had come to her immediately. She had been dreaming about her home being demolished… Casson had comforted her, making her forget her dream completely…

She caught her breath as she recalled the way he had ignited her with the gentle exploration of his lips and hands, the way her responses had made him bolder.

And she had done nothing to stop him.

She hadn't wanted to; she had luxuriated in

every masterful move he'd made, driving her to reciprocate just as passionately.

She retrieved his T-shirt and put it on, her limbs weak at the thought of Casson being in the kitchen. She wondered if he would be returning to the bedroom…

"Cass?" she said out loud, and then waited, her heartbeat accelerating.

A scuffle at the door seconds later along with a whimper made her smile.

"Good morning, Luna," she called out.

She waited for Casson's good morning, but all she heard was Luna pawing at the door. Justine opened it and Luna barged in, wagging her tail, and promptly jumped on the bed.

"I hope your master gave you permission to do that," Justine said, wagging her finger at Luna.

She peeked out the door, expecting to see Casson, but he wasn't there. She didn't hear the shower, or water running in the washroom, so where *was* he?

Justine walked to the door and looked out. His Mustang was gone. And she hadn't even heard it. Mystified, she walked into the kitchen. He must have only just left; the coffee was still dripping. *But why?*

Had last night meant so little to him that he could just take off like that? Or had something come up with Andy? Had Ronnie called with an emergency?

Her heart began to thud. And then she caught sight of her name on the piece of paper taped on the side of the coffee maker. She peeled it off, and praying it wasn't bad news, began to read…

Good morning, Justine.

I hope you had a good sleep. I'm sorry I couldn't stay, but I have some business to take care of. I'm heading to my home in Huntsville to pick up some things, and then I'll be in and out of the cottage before an event I need to attend tonight.

I meant to tell you about it, and you may have heard about it anyway. The Stockey Centre is holding an exhibition this week of the work of two of the Group of Seven artists. It's called Franklin & Casson on the Bay. It opens this evening. Please come.

I've already taken Luna out this morning,

and she's had her breakfast —don't let her tell you otherwise!

Please make yourself at home—I know; it is *your home!—and help yourself to coffee and the fabulous lemon blueberry muffins on the counter. A special friend made them.*
Casson
P.S. I would have really liked to have had breakfast with you, Justine...

He had added a happy face, and relief flooded her that Casson's leaving had nothing to do with Andy. But she couldn't help feeling disappointed at how impersonal the letter seemed. Until she got to the part where Casson called her "a special friend." Her heart skipped a beat at that. And his last line lifted her spirits tenfold.

It wasn't exactly a declaration of love, or passion, and he had made no reference to the time they had spent together—or *how* they had spent the time—but it told Justine one thing for sure: Casson would have remained at the cottage this morning if he could.

Which meant that he wasn't running away from her, and that the previous evening must have meant *something* to him. That maybe he might be wanting to continue spending time with her…

Feeling a little giddy with happiness, Justine poured herself a cup of coffee. She had already made up her mind; she was definitely going to see Franklin & Casson on the Bay!"

And the man she loved.

Casson rolled down the windows of his Mustang, enjoying the feel of the morning breeze as he exited the main highway and turned on to the country road leading to Huntsville. He smiled at the thought of Justine reading his note in the kitchen. He pictured her in his T-shirt, relaxing with a mug of coffee.

When had he realized that he loved her company, loved everything about her?

Falling in love had not been on his agenda. It hadn't even been on his wish list. But, despite their awkward start, he and Justine had more than made up for it.

His abdomen tightened at the memory of her body, soft and hard in all the right places. It would be sweet torture to be away from her for the entire day. He hoped she would be free to spend some time with him when he drove back to the cottage. And he hoped she would accept his invitation to come to the opening night of the exhibition. It was time she saw for herself what his resort venture was *really* about.

He'd wait until after the event to break the news about the deed, though. He couldn't predict her reaction, but if she felt the same about him as he felt about her—and he was sure that she did—he was confident that they could come up with a solution.

After tonight there would be no more secrets between them. Not that he had kept any information from her with the intention of gaining the upper hand. No, he had simply tried to assess what would be the appropriate time to reveal his real motive in wanting Winter's Haven. And when she would be most receptive to hearing the news about the deed.

It was time for Justine to know the truth. He had seen passion in her eyes, and his body had been rocked with the passion they had shared, but he was certain that what they had experienced was more than just physical. He was confident he had gained her trust.

Realizing that he had increased his speed in anticipation of seeing Justine, he eased his foot on the pedal. Getting a ticket now would just delay his return.

Patience, he told himself. *You're minutes away...*

He had been successful on one count. Now all he needed was Winter's Haven.

And Justine Winter.

Justine finished her muffin and coffee, gave a lazy stretch, and padded back to the bedroom. Luna followed, and Justine ruffled her fur affectionately. She sauntered to the window and opened the blinds fully, letting in the early-morning sun. Turning, she let her eye fall on the brown envelope on the dresser.

She pressed her lips together and picked it up. Casson had wanted to show her the documents inside it from the very beginning. And yesterday as well... She didn't suppose it would bother him if she went ahead and looked through it without him.

She brought the envelope into the living room and curled up on the couch. She took out the contents: a number of files separated by clips. She riffled through them quickly, her eyes registering survey documents and reports, a deed, architectural designs, and a typed letter.

Seeing her name in the salutation startled her, and she pulled the letter from the pile and started to read.

Dear Ms. Winter,

As you know, I have recently purchased the properties on either side of Winter's Haven from Mr. and Mrs. Russell. In perusing the documents I discovered that their ancestors—the pioneers who first owned the acreage that comprises both their and your properties—had partitioned the land and eventually sold the parcel that years later became Winter's Haven.

Well, a few generations have come and gone, and it seems that the original papers were misplaced. After the Russells sold to me, and started packing, the original deed turned up and they passed it on to me. I looked it over the other night and compared it to the surveyor's report I received when my transaction was finalized.

To make a long story short, it seems that a section of Winter's Haven is actually on the Russells' property.

"That's insane!" Justine blurted, letting out a hollow laugh before continuing to read.

I have verification that a section of your house and some of your property is actually sitting on what is now my property. You are welcome to check with your lawyer. I already have with mine.

The properties passed hands years ago, between neighbors and friends, and in one of those subsequent transactions a new survey report had to be drawn up when the original deed couldn't be located.

Justine clenched her jaw as she rifled through all the documents and reports. Her cheeks burned. She bit her lip.

This couldn't be true.

After poring over them a second time she sank

back against the couch, the truth turning her body cold.

I am willing to discuss the ramifications of this finding with you, and anticipate our working together to discuss options that will result in a mutually satisfying solution.

I am prepared to make a substantial offer for Winter's Haven, and would like to meet with you at your earliest convenience to present you with my plans for a resort development on the properties.

My contact information follows. I look forward to hearing from you.

Cordially yours,
Casson Forrester

Justine tossed the papers on the coffee table. The ice that had filled her veins as she read every word of Casson's letter was now changing to a flow of red-hot lava. She could still feel the burning in her cheeks, the roiling in her stomach. Her breaths were shallow and her chest was heaving, her lungs heavy with Casson's deceit.

How could he?

Why hadn't he shown it to her before? Or even

mailed it instead of playing games with her? Instead of manipulating his way into Winter's Haven after weaseling a deal with the Russells…

The Russells sold willingly.

Justine put her hands over her ears in an attempt to block that inner voice. Okay, so Casson had been proactive, jumping on an opportunity. The Russells had come over to her office to say their goodbyes, and had expressed their excitement at moving south to be with their daughter. Casson had made a decision that they had been waffling over very easy. His timing—and his offer—couldn't have been better, they'd said.

But keeping the deed a secret from her was despicable.

So what exactly did she plan to do about this? Justine tried to digest the fact that Casson had a claim on part of Winter's Haven. No wonder he was always so relaxed, even when she appeared unexpectedly at his door. It was as if he owned the place already…

Had she known this right from the beginning she wouldn't have ended up in his bed—that much she knew. Her stomach tightened as if she had been pummeled. Hot tears slid onto her cheeks and she bit her lip.

Casson had used her—manipulating her to get her under his control, working to soften her up so she would sell...

Her fists clenched. Robert had controlled her in one way—slowly building up their relationship while his marriage withered, and then dropping her when she no longer served his purpose. Justine had vowed never to let another man control her. And yet here she was, caught in the web that Casson had woven so meticulously. She had allowed herself to be manipulated yet again.

She could kick herself for being such a fool. How could she have let her guard down?

And how could she face Casson? He must be gloating inwardly. And what would he be expecting of her now? To give in and turn over the property, seeing how she'd so readily turned herself over to him?

Not a chance in hell.

Wiping the tears from her face, Justine stared blindly out the window. She took no pleasure from the view, her stomach twisting at memories of her and Casson in the bay. And of how thoroughly he had seduced her after her nightmare…

He had been just as bad, if not worse than Robert.

Holding her hand over her mouth, Justine fled to the washroom.

When Casson arrived at his house in Huntsville he wasted no time in gathering what he needed for opening night: suit, shirt, cufflinks, tie and shoes. He had already taken the A. J. Casson painting from his collection to the Stockey Centre when he had taken possession of the Russell properties.

He was anxious to get back to the cottage in time to look over his opening speech and have a few hours to himself before heading to the center. Well, not really to himself. He smiled. He wanted to see Justine. Invite her properly to the exhibition opening and the banquet.

He had goofed by not mentioning the banquet in his letter, but he hoped she would understand and accept. A surge of excitement shot through his body. He was already feeling high because his dream of a resort for children with cancer was about to kick off, and if Justine accompanied him to the opening event he'd be over the moon.

Casson pulled into a gas station and called the office at Winter's Haven. With any luck Justine would answer, and he'd ask her to meet him at his cottage…

"Hi, Mandy." He tried not to let his disappointment show in his voice. "Would Justine be in the office?"

There was silence, and Casson wondered if there was a problem with the connection.

"Oh…hi, Casson. She…she was in here earlier, but she went back home."

Casson frowned. Mandy's voice wasn't as cheery as usual. "Would you mind giving her a message? I'm on my way back and should be there in half an hour. I'd appreciate it if she could meet me at my cottage when she gets a chance…"

Another pause. Then, "Will do."

"Thanks." Casson turned off his phone.

He shrugged. Mandy must be having a bad day. Oh, well, in a very short time *his* day would be getting even better.

With a roar of his engine, he headed toward Parry Sound.

* * *

Justine bit her lip and tried not to cry as Mandy put the phone down. She had already spent an hour crying at home, before splashing cold water on her face and going to the office. She had said nothing to Mandy about spending the night with Casson; she felt too humiliated. The only thing she had shared was the information in Casson's letter about the property.

When Casson had called she had waved her arms frantically, so that Mandy wouldn't reveal that she was in the office. Now Mandy was looking at her worriedly.

"Justine, maybe you *should* go and meet him. He might have come up with a solution…"

Justine gave a bitter laugh. "If I didn't trust him before, I trust him even less now."

"But he said in the letter he wanted to discuss options. Just hear him out. At the very least you can tell him how you feel. I can understand that you're royally ticked off, Justine. But nothing will be resolved without talking to him."

Justine pursed her lips. Maybe she *did* need to tell Casson how she felt. She took a deep breath.

Yes, she decided, she would be meeting him at his cottage.

Prepared and ready to do battle.

Casson had let Luna out and was giving her a snack inside when he heard the sharp rap at the door. His heart did a flip when he saw it was Justine, but his smile froze on his way to get the door. There was no returning smile from her. In fact her eyes were puffy and red, her expression cold. She held her arms stiffly behind her back.

He opened the door. "Justine? Has something happened? What's wrong?"

Justine smirked. "Really?" She held up the envelope she had taken with her. "*This* is what's wrong." Her hand trembled. "You deliberately led me on in your scheme to get me to sell Winter's Haven, knowing the whole time that you already owned part of it." She clenched her jaw. "You could have given me the letter—or mailed it to me—*before*."

Casson glanced at the envelope and then back at her, temporarily stunned. "How...?"

He didn't need to finish.

He had left it on the desk.

"Look, Justine—"

"No, *you* look. What you did was despicable. You and Robert can shake hands. At least he was drunk and not in his right mind. But you knew what you were doing. You *knew*."

Casson's heart twisted.

How could he convince her she had it wrong?

"Justine, I swear I didn't plan it to work out this way—"

"You can't deny you had a plan." Her narrowed eyes shot ice daggers at him.

"Yes, I had a plan—but not the one you think. I planned to come to Winter's Haven, meet you in person, and try to sell you my idea for a resort. I found out about the deed *after* making arrangements to stay at this cottage. I was waiting for the right time to tell you about it."

Justine cringed. "And when *was* that? After getting me to sleep with you?"

A fist in the gut would have been easier to take than the disgust in her voice.

"Justine, I did not sleep with you because I had an ulterior motive. It was not in my 'plan.' What happened between us was not premeditated. I'm not that kind of a guy."

She opened her mouth as if she were ready to fire back a retort, then closed it.

"I never tried to take advantage of you, Justine. My feelings are genuine." He sighed. "But I know now that I should have told you about the deed right from the start."

Justine crossed her arms, her expression grim. "So what exactly are you prepared to do about it?"

"I'm prepared to have a discussion with you about options—"

"*What* options?" Justine said hotly. "I will need to consult a lawyer as to how the deed can be adjusted and…and…" Her jaw clenched, as if she'd realized it wasn't going to be a simple matter to rectify. Especially with part of a structure—her *home*—on his property. "I need to call my parents," she said, throwing her hands up in the air and staring up at the ceiling. "Maybe they'll know what to do."

Something shifted inside of Casson when he heard the hint of despair in her voice.

He didn't want to hurt her; he had never wanted to hurt her.

For the first time he realized how vulnerable she felt when it came to Winter's Haven.

"Look, Justine," he said softly, hoping to reassure her, "I'm not taking or claiming even a corner of your house or your land. Right now, I think the only option is to leave things the way they are." He leaned closer, forcing her to meet his gaze. "When we can come up with a satisfying solution for the both of us, *then* we'll do something about it. And update the deed."

"The only satisfying solution for *you* is to get me to sell you the business." Justine's voice was tinged with bitterness.

"There could be other solutions…and they may come to light before my holiday here comes to an end."

"And what if they don't?" Justine's voice held a challenge.

"We'll figure something out," Casson insisted. "Even if it means locking ourselves in a room together until we do."

Justine shot him a *you're out of your mind* look before handing him the envelope. "I've made a copy of everything to give to my lawyer," she said curtly. “And I’ve left another copy in the office with Mandy.”

She turned to leave.

“Justine.” He waited until she’d turned around. “I know you’re still upset, and you have every right to be, but I meant every word I said. I’m really sorry I hurt you.” His voice wavered. “You might think I’m crazy to even ask…but I’d really like you to come to the exhibition tonight.”

Justine’s jaw dropped and her eyes narrowed into two beams of fury. “You’ve *got* to be kidding.”

She walked stiffly out the door, letting it slam shut behind her.

CHAPTER NINETEEN

IN THE OFFICE, after giving Mandy a condensed version of the meeting she had had with Casson, Mandy asked if Justine would be going to the opening of the art show. Justine became flustered, and Mandy gave her a comforting hug.

"Just go," she urged. "Give the guy a chance. Let him talk to you when the shock has worn off..."

Back at home, Justine debated for two hours over whether or not she should go. She was still angry and hurt, not to mention bewildered as to what purpose Casson had in asking her to attend the opening.

She wanted to punish him by not accepting, but a tiny voice inside her told her she'd just be punishing herself. She remembered how happy she had been when Casson had suggested she go in his note... Besides, she was not going *with* him; she could stay as little or as long as she wanted. And she had to admit she *was* curious...

So she'd brace her broken heart and show Casson that she hadn't come undone as a result of his deception—that she was strong and capable of standing up to him. *That she wasn't under his control.*

Her mind was too clouded now to think of a solution to the deed issue, but she would contact her parents' lawyer in the morning and book an appointment as soon as possible. There *had* to be a way of voiding Casson's claim to Winter's Haven.

With a defiant toss of her head Justine went upstairs to look through her closet. The warrior in her was *not* defeated, she realized, her jaw clenching. She *would* go to Casson's event.

Dressed to kill.

Justine decided on a sleeveless black dress with a diagonal neckline, accented with filigree silver buttons. After styling her dark hair in soft flowing curls, she put on the dress. It hugged her curves and stopped above her knees. She chose a pair of silver dangling earrings with diamonds and sapphires—her parents' graduation gift. And finally she picked out a black shawl that shimmered with silver threads.

She was pleased when she saw her reflection, liking the way the sapphire stones matched her eyes.

She applied the barest amount of make-up—some delicate touches of blue and silver-gray eye-shadow, and a frosty pink lipstick. Blush wasn't necessary; her cheeks were already flushed.

She stepped into black pumps with silver stiletto heels and, grabbing her silver clutch purse, walked gingerly out to her car.

When Justine arrived at the parking lot of the Stockey Centre many spots were already filled. As she circled around her heart skipped a beat at the sight of a gleaming red car in a far corner.

Casson's Ferrari.

She sat for a moment after turning off the ignition, her hands gripping the wheel.

Did she really want to do this?

People were streaming into the building, being welcomed by a smiling doorman. Women with elegant dresses and glittering shawls, and bling that sparkled in the late-afternoon sun. Men sporting expensive suits and ties, their shoes gleaming.

Justine took a deep breath and climbed out of her car.

The huge foyer was buzzing with chatter. Justine had only taken a few steps when the people in front of her moved on to join their friends. It was then that Justine caught sight of the words Franklin & Casson on the Bay at the top of a huge banner stand. Her gaze dropped to the life-size image of two boys, grinning and holding up a fishing pole with their catch.

And then she froze when she realized that she was eye to eye with Casson. Not Casson the man, but Casson the boy. Her pulse quickened and her eyes flew to the boy next to him, with his two front teeth missing. *Franklin.* Her eyes began to well up. Squeezing them to clear her vision, she stared at the little boy who had passed away a year after this photo was taken.

Justine gulped. She had come to see paintings by Franklin Carmichael and A. J. Casson. The last thing she had expected to see was a huge image of Casson with his brother. It was heart-breaking. *But why had Casson done it?* She knew the connection between the brothers and the artists, but she'd had no idea that Casson would reveal something so personal to the public.

"Mr. Forrester couldn't have picked a better photo for this exhibition."

A guide with the name 'Charlotte' on her tag stood next to Justine. "The brothers on Georgian Bay. And what a beautiful tribute to Franklin—to plan a resort in his name."

"Resort?" Justine said, dazed.

"Yes. You must have heard about it in the news? Franklin's Resort. Mr. Forrester has purchased property in the area and is planning a luxury resort for children with cancer and their families to enjoy for a week after their final chemotherapy and radiation treatments. There will be no charge for them—which is why he is seeking support to augment his very generous contribution and to help keep the project viable."

She pointed to the registration table.

"There's a donation box on the table, and in the adjoining room Mr. Forrester has unveiled an A. J. Casson painting from his own private collection to be auctioned off tonight." She smiled at Justine. "Please sign your name in the guest book—and if you would like to receive information about future fund-raising events for the resort, please include your email address."

"Thank you," Justine managed to reply.

She glanced again at the faces of the brothers and thought of Andy. Feeling her eyes prickling, she quickly signed the guest book, put a few bills in the donation box and then, stifling a sob, turned away and started making her way through the throng to find the washroom, where she could get control of her emotions in private.

Halfway there, the tears started spilling out of her eyes. And then she bumped hard into someone and almost lost her balance, teetering on her stiletto heels.

"Justine."

Two arms came out to stop her from falling.

"I'm so glad you could come."

She recognized the deep voice even before looking up at tiger eyes.

Trembling, she fell against his chest and looked up at him with blurred eyes. *"Why didn't you tell me?"*

"It's complicated," Casson murmured in Justine's ear while helping her regain her balance. "I know where there's a quiet place to talk. *Please,*" he added, seeing her hesitate. "We need to talk."

"Mr. Forrester!" a voice called. "May we have a moment of your time?"

Casson turned and recognized a reporter from the local paper, striding toward him. Jake Ross. Beside him was the paper's photographer—Ken—who had already taken some photos of him next to the banner stand.

Casson smiled and nodded, before turning to Justine to tell her she didn't have to leave while they interviewed him. But she had already walked away and the crowd had closed in around her.

Damn!

Hiding his frustration, he checked his watch and led Jake and Ken to a quieter corner. He'd try his best to hurry things along. He wanted to clear things up with Justine before the banquet and auction.

While Jake interviewed him, asking all the questions Casson had expected to be asked, Casson kept glancing toward the crowd. He couldn't see Justine at first, and then a small group shifted to gather around a series of Casson paintings in order to hear the gallery owner's description of the pieces and he glimpsed her there, her lustrous hair framing her beautiful face.

Casson could hardly concentrate after that, taking in her little black dress from its slanted neckline to where it ended above her knees. Her legs were stunning in silky hose, and those shoes... His pulse couldn't help but race.

He heard Jake ask him a question twice, and forced himself to focus. Casson thanked Jake when the interview was over, and then the photographer asked to take some photos of Casson with the paintings.

"We want Casson next to the Cassons," he joked.

The gallery owner paused as they reached the group, and thanked the guests in advance for graciously waiting while the media did their job. Casson tried to catch Justine's eye, but she was deliberately keeping her gaze on one of the paintings. He stood in the center of the display, with paintings on either side of him, and patiently did what the photographer suggested.

"How about one with some of the guests?" Casson suggested, and placed himself impulsively next to Justine.

She looked up from the painting and raised her eyebrows at him with a *what do you think you're doing?* expression. Just then the photographer began to snap some pictures. Justine turned toward Ken at the first click, and Casson took the split-second opportunity to place his hand around Justine's waist and press her closer to him.

Another *snap* and Ken gave him a wink and a thumbs-up before sauntering off with Jake toward a large group at the Franklin Carmichael display.

Justine strode off in the opposite direction.

Casson quickly caught up.

"Why did you do that?" Justine muttered, glancing from him to all the people who were looking their way, and then back at him.

Even with a frown she was gorgeous. "Because I wanted my photo taken next to a beautiful woman," he said. "You look amazing, Justine." His eyes swept over her and he couldn't help smiling. "I was hoping you would come."

"Why?" Justine stared at him accusingly. "So you could make me feel guilty for not wanting to sell Winter's Haven when it's for such a good cause?"

Casson's smile faded. "I had no intention of making you feel guilty," he said quietly.

"Well, I *do*," Justine said, her voice wavering. "I—I wish you had told me from the beginning that your resort was to be a non-profit venture to help kids with cancer, and not for your own personal gain."

"You were dead-set against my proposal from the beginning," Casson reminded her. "I *wanted* to show you the plans, remember? I drove over to your place, but you weren't ready to see them or to hear me out…"

He moved to let someone go by.

"So I decided I needed to wait for the right time. I wasn't sure how long it would take, but I knew I had to try to find the opportunity to do so. And that's why I booked myself into Winter's Haven."

Casson looked over Justine's head at the crowd.

"Look, we can't talk here. Let's go outside. I know where there's a private exit."

He led Justine through a series of hallways to a door that he made sure stayed open a crack using his car keys. They walked out into a private courtyard with a view of the bay. The water was lapping gently against the rocky shore and a couple of seagulls swooped high above.

Casson stopped and gently took hold of Justine's elbow. "I wanted to tell you I don't know how many times," he said gruffly. "But the idea of talking about Franklin to you made me feel… too vulnerable."

He looked into Justine's eyes and knew he owed her complete honesty.

"I grew up suppressing the truth that my parents—my mother especially—were so devastated with losing Franklin that they forgot…forgot they had another son who was still alive."

He took a deep breath.

"They forgot that *I* was devastated too. I didn't show it, I guess. I tried to be the perfect son for them, so as not to cause them anymore grief, but being perfect wasn't enough to get them to really notice me. Don't get me wrong. I had a nice home, plenty of food, a great education. I didn't want for anything like that. What I wanted most was something that died inside of them when Franklin died."

Casson felt the backs of his eyes prickling.

"And maybe because of that I never knew if I

had the capacity to really love somebody other than Franklin."

"You love Andy and Ronnie."

"Yes, I do. And this resort is for Andy's sake, too." He heard his voice waver. "I wasn't able to do anything for Franklin, but I *can* help Andy and other children like him..."

He took Justine's hands and covered them with his.

"I came to Winter's Haven with one thought in mind, and then I found myself falling in love."

"It's not hard to fall in love with Winter's Haven."

"I meant with *you*, Miss Winter."

Casson realized that Justine's eyes were welling up too.

"I was waiting until I felt I could trust you with my feelings, Justine. Until I felt that you wouldn't be indifferent."

"Oh, Cass..." Justine wrapped her arms around him, pressing her head against his chest.

Casson felt something let go inside him. Those two words she had uttered told him everything.

He lifted her chin so she would meet his gaze. "When I found out about the property issue I intended to offer you some options—whether you wanted to sell or not. But something made me hold back. I eventually realized that the better option was to forget about trying to get you to sell, and focus instead on starting with a smaller resort on the Russells' main property. I planned to offer you a position as manager of Franklin's Resort, and then you could still manage Winter's Haven. At least I wouldn't lose *you*."

He gazed at Justine, and what he saw in her eyes made his heart leap.

"You won't lose me, Casson," she replied breathlessly.

Her eyes were shimmering as he pressed her closer to him. He kissed her gently, and as her lips moved to respond he deepened the kiss until they were both enflamed.

With ragged breathing, he pulled away reluctantly. "The banquet will be starting any minute," he said ruefully. "And I have to get myself under control." He took Justine's hand. "Come and join me. I'll have them add another place setting at my table."

Justine looked at him tenderly and shook her head. "No; this is *your* night, Casson. You need to focus on what you need to say. For Franklin's sake...and for kids like Andy." She planted a soft kiss on his lips. "I'll be waiting for you back home, Cass. With Luna-Lu."

He watched her walk away, his heart bursting, and then, with a lightness he couldn't remember feeling in a long time, he headed to the banquet room.

CHAPTER TWENTY

JUSTINE LEFT THE Stockey Centre with a sensation of wonder that made her whole body feel buoyant. She replayed Casson's words constantly in her head while driving home.

I found myself falling in love... With you, *Miss Winter.*

He loved her.

And his honesty tonight had made her anger and hurt disappear. Her humiliation at being used—gone! Casson loved her, body and soul, and she loved him the same way. And trusted him.

But maybe she hadn't told him in so many words.

Well, she would make up for it tonight.

Her heart had broken when he'd told her about his parents. She could only imagine how lonely he must have felt. Growing up in the shadow of his brother's death. Craving the attention and love of his parents, whose grief had stunted any relationship they could have had with their remaining son.

Thank goodness Casson hadn't taken the dark path to get noticed. Fallen in with the wrong crowd. Justine's heart swelled with pride, thinking of how Casson had studied and worked hard to make something of himself. And if he had gone unnoticed in his youth, he was certainly making up for it now.

How could she have ever lumped Casson and Robert into the same category? Who they were at their core was as different as dawn from dusk. Robert had acted in ways to satisfy his own ego, to benefit himself. Casson had been driven only by a selfless desire to use the resources he had to help children with cancer and to support their parents as well. And it wasn't a fleeting desire, but a lifelong intention. To honor his brother's memory.

Maybe she would have realized all this earlier, been open to Casson's vulnerability, if Robert's deception and her resulting distrust of him and other men hadn't influenced her judgment…

After leaving Casson, Justine had gone to take

a peek at the A. J. Casson painting in the silent auction room. She'd been curious to see what Casson had so generously donated to help boost his venture.

A security guard had stood at the entrance, and Justine had passed him in order to get to the center of the room, where the painting was being displayed. A few other people had been standing around, gazing at the large oil painting on canvas and murmuring to themselves. The other invited patrons must have already left to attend the banquet, she'd thought.

Storm on the Bay was breathtaking. A dark sky was streaked with indigo, gold and red, and the swirling waters reflected the colors like cut glass. On the hilltops, pines swayed in every direction, their distinctive Muskoka shape instantly recognizable.

Justine had almost gasped when she'd read that bidding was set to begin at three hundred and fifty thousand dollars. But this was a prime piece of work by a member of the Group of Seven.

As the guests had bustled about, Justine had heard an elderly woman saying to her husband, "Imagine Casson Forrester doing all this to help children with cancer, in honor of his little brother. Now, *that's* my idea of a true Canadian hero!"

Smiling, Justine had taken her leave. And now here she was, in the driveway of Cottage Number One. With her master key, she let herself in.

Luna's affectionate welcome almost brought her to tears. She took Luna out for a break, made sure she had enough fresh water, and gave her a treat.

"Just for being my BFF," she said, and laughed, giving her a pat.

Justine went into the bedroom. The T-shirt was still on the bed, but it wasn't folded the way she had left it. A flash of electricity surged through her as she imagined Casson picking it up when he got back earlier. Justine shivered as she slipped the T-shirt over her body and breathed in the lingering scent of Casson's cologne. Desire coiled throughout her as she thought about how Casson looked tonight, in a tailored black suit and maroon tie…

With a contentedness and anticipation she had never felt before, Justine snuggled into the bed. She started when Luna suddenly nudged the door open and bounded on top of the bed.

"Okay…for a little while, Luna-Lu." She chuckled, rubbing Luna behind the ears. "Until your papa comes home."

She dimmed the lamp on the night table and closed her eyes, happily imagining everything that might happen after Casson walked in the door…

Justine felt the bed vibrating and blinked in confusion. Luna had jumped off the bed and Justine turned over to see Casson framed in the doorway, gorgeous and grinning, his black suit jacket draped over one arm and his maroon tie loosened.

She positioned herself on her elbows and flashed him a wide smile. "How did it go, Mr. *Forrest?*"

As Casson strode toward her he took off his tie and flung his jacket on top of her clothes on the chair. And then he was sitting next to her, his eyes gleaming.

"A resounding success, Miss *Wintry.* The final bid for *Storm on the Bay* was a whopping nine hundred and fifty thousand dollars."

Justine felt like crying and shouting with joy at

the same time. She started to speak, but stopped when she felt her lips tremble. Her brow crinkled and a tear slid down her cheek.

"What's this?" Casson leaned forward and gently wiped her cheek.

He gazed at her so tenderly that Justine wanted to melt in his arms. She shifted to a sitting position and put her hands on his chest.

"I'm just happy for you," she said, fiddling idly with his cufflinks. "And for all the kids who are going to be able to stay at the resort one day. I… I thought about what you said before, Cass, and…and I will gladly accept your offer to manage Franklin's Resort."

Casson took her hand and slipped it underneath his shirt. The feel of his chest muscles and the beating of his heart made her pulse leap. She gazed into his eyes while he undid the rest of his buttons. And then, with a groan, he removed his shirt and wrapped his arms around her, kissing her with a passion that matched hers.

They fell back onto the bed, and Justine savored the firmness of his lips on hers. She ran her fingers through his hair and cupped the back of his head as his kiss deepened. She shivered as he kissed a path down her neck, sending flickers of heat through her. He stopped suddenly, and Justine's eyes flew open.

She watched in bewilderment as he got off the bed and began to kneel down on the rug beside the bed.

"Skedaddle, Luna," he ordered, and with a low grumble Luna got up and padded out of the room.

And there he was, on one knee, bare-chested, hair tousled from her touch, looking at her with those sexy, intense tiger eyes.

"What about my other offer?" he said huskily.

Justine frowned. *What other offer had he made?*

"I don't understand…"

Casson's eyes glinted. "The offer to be my wife."

He brought her hands up to kiss them, his gaze locking with hers.

"I love you, Miss Winter, and I would be honored if you'd accept my proposal to spend the rest of your life with me. I promise I won't pressure you about selling. Winter's Haven is yours, and I respect that. I'd be happy to develop only the Russell properties—*my* properties—for Franklin's Resort."

Justine breathed deeply, her heart ready to

burst. “I rather think Winter and Forrester go hand in hand, don’t you? Maybe we could change Winter’s Haven to Winter’s Forrest Haven. As for the offer to be your wife…” Her voice softened. “I accept, Mr. Forrester. And I love *you*.”

She pulled at his hands and a smile spread across her face.

“Now, get up here, Cass, and let’s seal the deal!”

EPILOGUE

CASSON LEANED BACK on the love seat with his arm around Justine. *His wife.* They had dimmed the lights and were gazing at the twinkling colored lights on the Christmas tree. Tinsel glittered from every tip, and the vintage Christmas ornaments that Justine had bought added to the brilliance.

He sniffed the air appreciatively. Justine had stuffed a turkey, and the aroma of it roasting, along with root vegetables and stuffing, was making his mouth water.

Ronnie and Andy would be arriving soon, to share their Christmas Eve dinner and to stay for a few days. Andy had been given a clean bill of health five months earlier, and had started to look more robust. His hair had grown in nice and thick, too.

Casson smiled. He couldn't wait to take him snowshoeing and ice-fishing. And skating on the

y. He had had a section cleared off for Andy to enjoy, with the new skates and helmet he would be giving him for Christmas, among the other things Ronnie had said Andy was wishing for.

Mandy and her fiancé were also on their way. They had set their wedding date for September, and were happily making plans. Justine's mom and dad were currently enjoying the heat in Australia, but had promised they would return to Winter's Haven in time for the baby's birth.

Casson put one hand on Justine's tummy and suddenly had a feeling of *déjà-vu.*

He had visualized this moment before...

His eyes sought Justine's—as blue-gray as the sky—and he gave a soft laugh.

"What's so funny, Cass?"

"I just remembered that I imagined a moment like this some time ago—when you were roasting marshmallows with Andy..."

She pursed her lips and he couldn't resist leaning forward to kiss her. *Thoroughly.*

When they drew apart, he saw that her eyes had misted.

"You and knowing we are going to have this baby are the best Christmas presents I could have ever hoped for or dreamed of," he murmured, stroking her head. "And when he or she is born in the summer, before the grand opening of Franklin's Resort, I'll be the happiest dad and man alive."

"Whether it's a boy or a girl?" She flashed him a grin.

"Whether it's a boy or a girl," he said solemnly, bringing her hand to his lips.

"We'll have to think about some names…" She cuddled up against him, placing her hand over his heart.

"Look, Justine!" He suddenly pointed toward the bay window. "A blue jay in the closest spruce tree."

He took her hand and led her to the window.

Justine caught her breath. "It's like a snow globe," she murmured. "How magical."

The snowflakes had been drifting down gently since early morning, and the evergreens were now padded with a soft quilt. The blue jay flitted from bough to bough, emitting its shrill cry and scattering snow like fairy dust. Its color was even more brilliant than usual against the dazzling white backdrop.

"How about Jay?" Casson said suddenly.

Justine's brow wrinkled as she gazed up at him.

"Jay…if it's a boy?"

Justine cocked her head at him. "I had a favorite doll called Amy. I was going to suggest Amy if it's a girl…"

The blue jay flew directly past the bay window.

Casson took both her hands, his tawny eyes blazing into hers. "I've got it! How about Amy Jay if it's a girl?"

Justine's heart flipped as she realized what Casson was getting at. *"A. J.,"* she whispered. "Oh, Cass, what a perfect name. I think Franklin would have approved." She placed a hand on her belly. "I have a feeling it'll be a girl…"

"And I have a feeling I'm in heaven," he said, and pulled her into his arms.

* * * * *